DEADLY NIGHT

DEADLY NIGHT

Christine Green

Severn House Large Print
London & New York

This first large print edition published in Great Britain 2007 by
SEVERN HOUSE LARGE PRINT BOOKS LTD of
9-15 High Street, Sutton, Surrey, SM1 1DF.
First world regular print edition published 2005 by
Severn House Publishers, London and New York.
This first large print edition published in the USA 2007 by
SEVERN HOUSE PUBLISHERS INC., of
595 Madison Avenue, New York, NY 10022.

British Library Cataloguing in Publication Data

Green, Christine
    Deadly night. - Large print ed. - (A Kate Kinsella mystery)
    1. Kinsella, Kate (Fictitious character) - Fiction 2. Women
    private investigators - Great Britain - Fiction
    3. Detective and mystery stories 4. Large type books
    I. Title
    823.9'14[F]

    ISBN-13: 978-0-7278-7586-0

Printed and bound in Great Britain by
MPG Books Ltd, Bodmin, Cornwall.

One

Winter settled quickly over Longborough, bringing with it harsh winds and rain. For days the only people braving the weather were those who had no choice.

The High Street bereft of shoppers had the look of a film set depicting some dreadful calamity. Shop lights resolutely glowed on to empty pavements and, as darkness fell earlier each day, the population seemed to hibernate.

Discontentment seemed everywhere, fuelled by poor weather and worries about everything from house prices to immigration. Television programmes featuring the joys of living in sun-filled foreign lands increased the sense of dissatisfaction. In idyllic settings, the wine flowed, there was time for lying on the beach and intimate dinner parties, everyone was welcoming and the 'locals' were kind and helpful. Dreams were dreamt but the majority toiled on, the sunny uplands and private pool forever beyond their grasp.

I continued to run my private investigation agency, once entitled Medical and Nursing Investigations, from my office above my landlord and friend Hubert Humberstone's funeral business. As an ex-nurse, I'd thought I could specialize, but I soon realized I was merely limiting my options. Hubert's business, in contrast, is more constant, only the weather being a major variable. The cold and the damp had taken its toll of the frail and elderly, and Hubert was busily advertising for more staff, but without much success.

My only job offer in the last two weeks had been to find a missing cockatiel, which I apologetically declined. I share ownership of a small terrier called Jasper, which means I know what a hold a pet can have on the heart. But I hadn't any idea how to find a missing bird and it would have been immoral to take money and give hope where there was none.

My house in Farley Wood, a small village just outside Longborough, is rented by an ex-client of mine, Megan, and my goddaughter Katy. My mother Marilyn has once more reverted to type and gone walkabout. This was after a short period of domesticity that proved to be too much for her to sustain. I had a postcard this week from Jamaica. Her message read: '*Have met a gorgeous man – Rommell Jackson. He's 23!*

Don't worry, I'm not planning to marry him. Just having fun. Love, Mum xxx. PS. He hasn't asked me yet.'

I hoped Rommell Jackson wasn't expecting to be kept in the lap of luxury, because my mother couldn't afford to feed or house a gerbil. I half-expected her to write again pleading for money. If that happens, I shall refuse, I told myself firmly, but I wasn't convinced that I would.

My only real ambition at the moment is to lose weight, because I'm finding size four-teens are being made smaller or I'm shrinking my clothes in the tumbledryer. Either way, I need to improve my image. My hair at the moment is natural blonde, at least, that's what it said on the packet, and the style is 'deconstructed', in other words, I haven't seen a hairdresser in yonks. But not long enough to forgive the bitchy comments from a very camp hairdresser. 'Well, dear, so many lovely colours in your hair and such varying lengths. Been at it yourself, have we?' Still, I'd have to steel myself, because one day my prince would come, and I wanted to look my best for when he did.

Life, being its usual bitchy self, means that none of the three attractive men I met on my last case have phoned me. One not phoning, I could understand, but three! I'm trying not to get a complex.

On Monday morning I sat in my office trying to plan my day. Outside, the rain dribbled relentlessly from a grey sky. I felt as motivated as a dying wasp, but I thought as long as I kept at my desk, inspiration would come knocking. Instead it was Hubert who came knocking on my door.

I knew by the expression on his face that he was worried. Not that a stranger would notice. He had a face befitting an undertaker, with solemn dark eyes, rapidly balding hair, which he tried to plaster down into strands, and a general air of world-weariness. Today, though, he was more world-weary than usual.

'I wouldn't ask,' he said, 'but there's no one else.'

I experienced a sinking feeling.

'Alice is off sick,' he explained. 'I've got three funerals today and I need help. Only a small job.'

My stomach sank towards my knees. 'There's no need to look so pained,' he said. 'You've got the time.'

'I'm busier than I look.'

'Come off it,' he snapped. 'You're just sitting there on your backside doing sod all.'

Now I was a little taken aback. Hubert was often mildly irritated by me, but not to this level. So I reasoned he wasn't exaggerating that he needed help. 'What do you want me to do?'

'I want you to get Mrs Ivy Waites ready for the chapel of rest. She's ninety-two, died at home from pneumonia. Her husband's in a local nursing home, he's a mere eighty-eight, and he wants to see her – today. One of the carers from the home is bringing him in by taxi in just over an hour. He's heartbroken and she looks – untidy. There's a dress for her to wear...' He broke off and looked at me with the same pleading expression that Jasper can manage. I was bored and it seemed churlish to refuse. After all, Hubert had bailed me out on many occasions and one little favour was all that he was asking. I'd always tried to maintain a distance from the activities of 'below', but a pleading look and I was unable to say no. A couple of drinks usually have the same effect, but this time it was in a good cause.

I followed him down to the 'cold room' and two of the driving staff carried out the coffin to an anteroom just off the chapel of rest. There Mrs Ivy Waites was gently lifted on to the purple cloth of the trolley. Hubert pointed me in the direction of a table that looked like the make-up kit of a movie star.

'A bit of concealer and foundation,' he said, 'and pad the cheeks out with cotton wool. Be subtle, Kate – we want the old boy to recognize her.' I didn't say a word. He

9

handed me a white New Testament with gold lettering; 'She wants to be buried with her christening Bible.' Then he showed me the dress she was to wear, together with a slip and silk knickers. In hospital, deceased patients were sent to the mortuary washed and dressed in nightclothes or a shroud. I'd never given much thought to what the average person might wear for their funeral. Mafia bosses, I knew, were often viewed in an open coffin wearing their best suits. Were they wearing Calvin Klein underpants? It didn't matter; it was just one of life's little mysteries. Ivy Waites would be wearing her best silk knickers and that was her wish. Would I care, when and if I reached ninety-odd? I didn't know. Best have a good pair in reserve, I decided, just in case.

When Hubert and the staff left me, I took a proper look at Ivy. Her face was a blue-grey colour; her eyes were sunken and thankfully well closed. Her white hair hung lankly to her shoulders, long and wispy except for a short tuft on her right temple. I looked at it more closely. It bothered me. It had been cut. Maybe it irritated her and she'd cut it herself. I lifted her hands – they were knobbly with arthritis and the skin so transparent all her veins showed like rivers on a relief map. Not hands that could easily wield scissors.

I took a large white towel from a pile by the make-up table and laid it lengthwise over her. Her modesty wasn't going to be affected, but old training dies hard, and as I began to remove her pink nightie, I kept up a running commentary. All the usual stuff. 'There we are. This arm first. Soon be more comfortable. That's it, up a bit.' It obviously didn't do much for Ivy but it made me feel better.

From the look of the sagging skin of her arms, she had once been a much larger woman. She'd come to Humberstone from her home and she hadn't been washed. Spittle had dried around her mouth, and food had settled in her bony clavicles. I found a bowl and a pile of flannels on a shelf under the sink. I filled the bowl with hot water but the only soap I could find was Fairy washing-up liquid. 'Never mind, Ivy,' I said. 'This stuff is meant to be kind to the skin.' I began washing her face and, when I'd washed her top half, I put on her slip easily enough and again covered her top half with a towel. 'I'll wash down below now, Ivy,' I said. I was just about to start soaping her when I noticed the bruises. On the insides of her thighs. I paused, taken aback. Not quite believing what I was seeing.

'What on earth happened here, Ivy?' I asked. Had she been roughly handled after death, I wondered? Not by Humberstone

11

staff, I was sure of that. The light in the ante-room was from a fairly dim long-life bulb. I needed a torch. I covered Ivy up with another towel and left her, rushed up to Hubert's kitchen, found his large torch and rushed back down again. Why I was rushing I don't know. It wasn't as if Ivy would die of pneumonia.

With the torch, I could see the bruises properly. They were finger marks, or more accurately fingers and thumbs. I felt sickened. Her husband was coming to see her, so she had to be ready. Hubert was conducting a funeral. The only thing I could do was abandon washing and dress her.

I hoped I was jumping to the wrong conclusion. The bruises appeared to be a few days old. I pulled up her silk knickers and picked up her pink floral dress. As I did so, a pair of sheer stockings fluttered to the floor. It was then I realized I should have worn gloves. I was bound to snag them. I apologized in advance and carefully fitted the stockings over her hammer toes and up her long skinny legs.

Once she was dressed I brushed her hair and fixed it into a neat roll with kirby grips. There was nothing I could do about the tuft of hair, only fix it with a little water. Then I dampened two wads of cotton wool and inserted them inside her cheeks. Her mouth seemed fixed into a rictus above her false teeth, so I had to rearrange her lips. After that, she looked much better. I chose a light foundation and, once I'd finished and added the merest hint of blusher, she looked ... healthy. Her blue lips I managed to disguise with a tiny smear of red lipstick. Finally I placed her christening Bible on her chest and crossed her hands over it. 'There you are, Ivy,' I said. 'All ready, and you look lovely.' And she did. The pink floral dress had a white collar and it framed her face beautifully.

I said nothing about the bruises to the drivers who wheeled her into the chapel of rest. That was for Hubert's ears alone. Once in the coffin, with her head on a silk cushion, Ivy finally looked at peace, and Bill, one of the drivers, said, 'You've done a good job, Kate. She looks as fit as a fiddle.'

Half an hour later, husband Walter was wheeled into Humberstone's by a teenage carer with a scared look and a nervous manner. Walter was a tiny man, almost dwarfed by his wheelchair. He wheezed and coughed and I doubted he would see the month out himself.

'I'll take him in,' I said to the carer. 'If you want?'

'Thanks. I've never been in one of these places before.'

The receptionist – yet another new one – had worked at Humberstone's for only a few weeks, but she was experienced and, more to the point, wore high-heeled shoes. A fact that weighed heavily in her favour, because Hubert had a penchant for skyscraper heels. Her name was Joy, which was lucky, because she had a cheerful nature and she was good with the parrot that lived in the front office. All in all, Hubert had found a treasure in Joy. Although she did have large teeth, was over six feet tall and came to work on a Harley Davidson. I had to admit she looked impressive in her leathers, and I had once caught Hubert caressing her boots in the staff room. She'd been widowed twice, so she knew the score, and I supposed she was in her fifties. An ideal age for Hubert.

'Pet, you come and sit with me and the parrot,' Joy said to the carer. 'And we'll have a cup of coffee.'

I wheeled Mr Waites into the chapel of rest. 'Married sixty years,' he wheezed. 'Sixty years...' He broke off as tears trickled down his face. 'I haven't seen 'er for weeks.' I patted his hands and parked him at the head of the coffin. Unfortunately he was so short that he could hardly see above the coffin. 'You'll 'ave to 'elp me stand up, duck. I can't see her properly.' I moved behind him, put both my arms under his and at the same time kicked the wheelchair back. He was slightly shorter than me but heavier than he looked. I struggled to keep him upright. He was still wheezing and struggling for breath but, as he clasped her hands, he said, 'She looks so bonny. Lovely woman...' He paused to cough. I struggled to hold him up. 'She only 'ad one fault,' he wheezed. 'Bloody religious fanatic she was, but she was a good wife.' He paused to gasp for breath. 'Now, don't you worry, my duck, I'll be with you soon.' He leant over to kiss her cheek and then staggered back. I clung on to him with grim determination and with one hand managed to grab the wheelchair. He collapsed back into the chair and I was left red-faced with the effort. His breathing seemed calmer after a few moments, but a single tear crept from his left eye. As I wheeled him out, he murmured croakily, 'I feel peaceful now. Thanks, love.'

The carer took over responsibility for Walter and his wheelchair, she kissed his cheek and he managed a smile. 'Will it be all right if my mate, Annie, comes to see Ivy,' she said. 'She was her morning carer.'

'Fine. Can she come soon?'

'Yeah. I'll give her a bell.'

She took out her mobile phone from the pocket of her blue uniform trousers and rang Annie. 'She'll be about an hour. That be

OK?'

'Fine.'

Their taxi arrived a few minutes later and Joy and I waved them off. 'That did him the world of good,' said Joy. 'Fancy a cuppa?'

An hour later, I was in reception waiting for Annie's arrival. I heard the crashing of gears and watched from the front door as she made a real performance of backing in a battered Ford Escort. Annie was short and bouncy, in her twenties, with a long ponytail and a nose stud. 'Thanks for letting me see her,' she said. 'I was her carer for two years. She was no trouble, always cheerful – not like some. Except for...' She broke off. 'Well ... when she became really ill.'

In the chapel of rest, Annie stared at Ivy's body. 'It doesn't look like her. She looks – great.' After a few moments, she patted Ivy's hands and murmured, ''Bye, love. You're in a better place now.'

'Did anything happen before Ivy became ill?' I asked, trying to sound really casual.

'Funny you should say that,' said Annie thoughtfully. 'I knew her quite well. I'd wash and dress her in the mornings and sit her in her chair. She managed to get to the downstairs loo – only a few yards – on her Zimmer frame. She had meals on wheels and I'd come again in the evening to put her to bed. On Friday morning when I came, she was wearing a different nightie. And she seemed upset. Said God had forsaken her. I suppose that was the pneumonia.'

'Probably,' I said. 'What about her hair?'

Annie looked at me sharply. 'I didn't do it,' she said defensively.

'Could Ivy have done it herself?'

She shook her head. 'She couldn't raise her arms or manage scissors because of her arthritis.'

'Who could have done it, then?'

Annie shrugged. 'I dunno. Her niece visited once a month, but that was two weeks before. The vicar came occasionally when she wanted Holy Communion. The doctor visited once a month and I came twice a day.'

'Seven days a week?' I queried.

'Yeah, I need the money.'

I paused and took a breath. I knew my next question would upset her. 'What about the bruises?' I asked.

She stared back at me in surprise. 'What bruises? I haven't seen any bruises. We're taught to check our clients for any skin problems or bruises and report them. I didn't see any fresh bruises. She does bruise easily, so I'm always really gentle with her.'

'These are at the tops of her thighs. Finger and thumb marks.'

Annie's hand went to her mouth. 'Oh my

17

God!' she murmured. 'That explains it.'

'Explains what?'

'On Thursday morning when I went to wash between her legs, she yanked the towel down and snatched the flannel from me and said she'd do it herself. It was a real struggle, because she couldn't grip the flannel properly. But she insisted. She'd never done that before. I mean, she wasn't embarrassed or anything – she'd known me too long.'

'What about the next day?'

Annie, by now, was looking pale and anxious. 'On Friday she seemed quite poorly and she only let me wash her hands and face. She refused to see the doctor, but on Saturday morning I called her own GP. He came to see her and listened to her chest and said he thought she had pneumonia, and started her on antibiotics. On Sunday morning when I arrived, she was dead in bed. Dr Little had said I could ring anytime if I was worried, so I rang him and he came and signed the death certificate and called Humberstone.'

'What do you think of Dr Little?'

'He's really caring but ever so doddery. He's past retirement age.'

We stood in silence for a few moments, both trying to put two and two together and not make it four. 'You don't think...' said Annie. 'You don't think...' she began again.

'I do think,' I said.

Annie by now looked tearful. Neither of us wanted to say the word. 'Poor, poor Ivy,' she said. Then she added, 'What are we going to do? They won't be able to bury her, will they?'

'Mr Humberstone will sort it out,' I said, but I had a fleeting shiver down my back.

We took a last look at Ivy. She wasn't going to be allowed to rest in peace. I had a feeling this was just the beginning. Something sinister and evil had happened in Longborough, and the someone responsible was out there ... waiting.

Two

Annie refused coffee but gave me her mobile number, and as she looked at my business card, her expression said it all – *What, you?* She walked away from Humberstone's dejected and not a bit bouncy. 'Is she all right?' asked Joy as she watched Annie drive away. 'She'll be OK,' I said. Joy peered at me above her reading specs. 'Is there something wrong?'

I forced a smile. 'I need to see Hubert, that's all.'

'He'll be about half an hour. He'll be ever so pleased with the way you've coped.'

'We'll see,' I said. 'Could you make sure Ivy's left where she is for the moment?'

Joy nodded but she was obviously a tad suspicious. 'You go upstairs, Kate, and make yourself a hot toddy. You look as if you need it.'

In Hubert's kitchen, I did gaze with a feeling of longing at the only alcohol there – a bottle of cooking sherry and a half bottle of two-day-old red wine. I looked at my watch.

Drinking and watching morning TV was akin to being in an Internet chat room – a pastime for those who had nothing better to do. Supremely dangerous for someone who works from home. The next step being not to bother to get dressed.

Luckily my urge for a drink faded as soon as I saw Hubert in the doorway.

'You should stop creeping up on me,' I said. 'I was lost in thought.'

'What about?'

'I fancied a drink but it's a bit early.'

'Well, you did a good job on Ivy. She looks at least ten years younger.'

'It's Ivy that I want to talk to you about.'

'The first time is always a bit difficult,' he said. 'You'll get used to it.'

'That was a one-off. I don't intend to get used to it.'

'You're a bit snappy,' he said. 'Is it your lunchtime? We could have a nice pub lunch that'll sort you out.'

Hubert thinks a new pair of shoes or a pub lunch is the answer to all life crises. This time he was wrong.

'There's a problem,' I said. 'With Ivy.'

'What sort of problem?'

'A contributory factor in her death.'

He frowned worriedly. 'Come on out with it. Then we can eat.'

I paused and the desire for a swig of

21

alcohol returned. 'I think she was raped three days before she died.'

Hubert's mouth opened and closed in surprise. 'What makes you think that?'

'She has finger and thumb bruises at the tops of her thighs and her carer reports that she behaved oddly and out of character in those three days.'

'Didn't the doctor notice?'

'He only examined her chest when he visited and then he came to sign the death certificate. It seemed like a natural death of a ninety-two-year-old.'

'I need a drink,' said Hubert.

We swooped on the cooking sherry, which tasted foul but very medicinal. 'You're positive those bruises are finger marks?' he asked between swigs.

'Yes. I checked them with a torch.'

'I'll ring the police,' he said. 'There'll have to be a post-mortem. The funeral will have to be cancelled and the friends and relatives informed.'

'I'm sorry, Hubert.'

'Don't be sorry. It's not your fault. That's what funeral directors are for – to make sure everything is above board.'

The police came an hour later. Slight over-kill, I thought, with sirens and a posse of uniforms and CID. The man in charge was Detective Chief Inspector Ray Waterworth.

He had a tendency to mumble and a disconcerting moustache which, together with a stocky frame and slicked-back dark hair, gave him an uncanny resemblance to Adolf Hitler. Although I don't suppose Hitler mumbled very often.

I accompanied the chief to the chapel of rest, where the rest of his entourage stood around looking as uncomfortable and as useful as novice priests in a brothel. CDI Waterworth muttered at me whilst seeming transfixed by Ivy. Since I didn't understand a word he said, I too stood there gormlessly staring at Ivy. The next time he mumbled, I understood, especially as he handed me a pair of surgical gloves. I didn't want to tell him I hadn't used gloves whilst preparing Ivy, but I slipped them on and did as I was told.

'Show me the bruises,' he said again. Mentally I nicknamed him 'Twice Waterworth'. I realized now that his accent was vaguely Scots. A sort of strangulated Glaswegian. I guessed his mother was the Scot.

'It does look suspicious,' he said. 'She'll need a post-mortem.'

I supplied him with Annie's mobile number and he ignored me from then on, and spoke to a small group who'd congregated near the door. It was as I was slinking away I heard someone say – 'Bit like the last one, sir.' To which Waterworth answered, with no trace of a mumble, 'Bollocks, man.' And then for good measure repeated it.

Half an hour later, Ivy's body was driven to the hospital morgue in one of Humberstone's hearses.

After that, Hubert made several phone calls. He cancelled the vicar, informed the nursing home that Ivy's funeral had had to be delayed because the grave diggers were on industrial action. I thought his ingenuity was top notch, but would it work? And was it fair on the grave diggers? He rang Ivy's niece and the vicar of the church Ivy had attended for many years. Eventually he had informed everyone who needed to know, including Ivy's GP, Dr Little, and then we walked to the Crown for a pub lunch. It wasn't my favourite pub but Hubert was a fan of their steak and kidney pies. Feeling virtuous, I ordered a tuna-filled jacket potato.

We sat in a gloomy corner of the pub and I told Hubert I'd heard a snippet of conversation that indicated Ivy was not the only one. 'I hope you're wrong,' he said. 'Longborough's always been a quiet town.'

It was five days later that Longborough changed its status.

I'd been cooking our Sunday-morning

24

breakfast and trawling the radio stations trying to avoid turgid church services when a local radio station announced that an eighteen-year-old girl had been found battered to death in her garden shed. Her parents had reported her missing at twelve thirty a.m. when she failed to return from visiting a girlfriend. Her father had found her body at seven a.m.

'What's up?' asked Hubert as he walked into the kitchen followed by Jasper and wearing what looked like a dressing gown circa 1903 – blue velvet with a thick gold cord around his waist. Jasper lunged at my legs and I stroked his head for a few moments before replying, 'An eighteen-year-old girl has been found battered to death in her garden shed.'

'Where?'

'Here in Longborough. Chorley Avenue.'

'Oh my God,' he muttered as he sat down.

We ate the breakfast I'd cooked, even though neither of us enjoyed it. I have to admit, a murder less than half a mile away is a chilling experience. At first the implications aren't that clear, but they became all too clear when Hubert announced, 'No walking Jasper on your own in the dark. Either I'll do it or I'll come with you.'

'That's going a bit far,' I said. I glanced at Jasper, who lay at Hubert's feet with his ears cocked.

'I don't think so,' Hubert said sharply. 'There's a murderer on the loose in Long-borough and, until they're caught, no woman is safe, especially after dark.'

Even worse, I thought grimly, was the fact that there could be both a rapist and a murderer. I'd heard of men who only raped old ladies, but I supposed there were men out there whose violence knew no barriers. Suddenly 'out there' was far too close for comfort.

'And another thing,' said Hubert, standing up and wagging a finger at me. 'Don't get involved – professionally, I mean.'

'I'm hardly likely to, am I? I should think police will be drafted in from all over the country.'

'A bit early yet for that,' he said. 'But I don't expect it will be long before they catch him. DNA catches a good few criminals these days.'

On that positive note, Hubert left the kitchen with Jasper at his heels, and I stared into space for a while.

The ring tone of my office phone echoed loudly in the quiet of Sunday morning. I rushed upstairs thinking it might be a job offer or some long-lost man. It was neither. It was Annie sounding upset. 'Could you see me this afternoon when I've finished work for today? I've got something to tell you.'

'Here?' I asked.

'No. I can't leave the house,' she said. 'Could you come to me?'

She gave me the address, a year-old council estate on the edge of town. 'I'll be there about three.'

'Thanks.'

She sounded depressed and I wondered if there was any police news. Since Ivy had been taken away, it was as if she'd gone into some void. Hubert, I knew, had tried to persuade the police to give him a date that Ivy could be buried, but it seemed that was impossible 'at this stage in our enquiries'.

The Pines council estate, although a Longborough 'afterthought', so far out of town it was almost rural, had been built on the edge of a pine wood. The houses were small but the gardens were neat and it didn't shriek 'council'.

Annie opened the door with a sleepy baby in her arms. I supposed the baby was about six months old. 'You're a dark horse,' I said. 'She's beautiful. What's her name?'

'He's called Sean.'

The living room smelt of baby oil and baby. Annie had gone for a Mediterranean theme, with terracotta walls and prints of whitewashed Spanish towns. Tall green plants made a backdrop for three shelves of Spanish jugs and dolls.

'It's like being in Spain,' I said, as I eagerly removed my coat in the oppressive heat of the central heating.

'Yeah, I like it warm.'

She looked down at the beautiful Sean, who had unusually long eyelashes. He was obviously asleep. 'I'll take him upstairs,' she said.

Moments later she reappeared and suggested coffee. 'Come on, I'll show you the kitchen.'

The kitchen too reflected a Spanish theme with a tiled floor and cream and terracotta splashbacks. There was enough room for a small pine table and two chairs. In the middle of the table was a bowl of artificial oranges. Annie placed a large mug of coffee in front of me. 'It's lovely, this house,' she said. 'Best place I've ever lived in. When I'm here, the sun always shines – like in Spain.'

'Is Spain your favourite place?' I asked.

'Dunno. I've never been there. I did do a GCSE in Spanish.'

Annie sipped at the scalding coffee. She looked tense. 'What's wrong, Annie,' I asked. There was a pause before she answered. A long pause. 'It's about Ivy's door key.'

'What about it?'

'I told her not to leave it there, but she

wouldn't take any notice.'

'A spare key, was it?'

'Yeah. She'd had it hidden before she had me as her carer. She was like a lot of old people. She didn't trust neighbours she hadn't known for years. The couple next door had been there for five years, but she still preferred to leave her key under a flowerpot.'

'What's the problem? It was her choice.'

'The agency likes us to have a key or access to a key, but they don't like the idea of hidden keys or keys on string hanging inside the front door.'

'And so you think the rapist found the key and let himself in.'

'I keep blaming myself. I shouldn't have let her keep the key there.'

'Maybe she let him in,' I suggested. 'She could walk on her Zimmer frame, couldn't she?'

'Yes. But she wouldn't have opened the door to a stranger...' She broke off, realizing that maybe her attacker hadn't been a stranger. 'It's scary, isn't it?' she said.

I nodded in agreement. 'You must be careful at night,' I said.

'There's another thing I'm worried about.'

'What's that?'

'She had money all over the place. How will the police know if she was robbed? Perhaps the money was the reason he attacked her.'

'The police will have to deal with that,' I said.

'The key is still bothering me,' said Annie, frowning. 'The police ought to know about it.'

'But you don't want to tell them?'

'They asked me already and I lied. I just said I had a key and her niece had a key and I didn't know if there were any other keys.'

'Maybe they've already found it.'

'What if they haven't? He could come back to the house. Attack someone else.'

'You're worrying too much, Annie. We have to trust the police to get it right.'

'You say that,' Annie snapped back. 'But what about the teenager who was found dead in her garden shed this morning?'

'That had nothing to do with a key.'

Annie shrugged despondently and I tried hard to think of something to lift her spirits.

'One thing I could do,' I said, 'is check that the key is still there – or, if it isn't, I'll try to find out from someone I know in the police force.'

'And what about her money?' she asked. 'I'm always worried when one of my patients dies with money all over the place.'

I knew immediately what she meant. Relatives often came along suggesting that they expected there to be more money, and the carer was first in line in the suspicion stakes.

Annie's expression was now more despondent than ever. 'I haven't told anyone else this, and I'm telling you in confidence – please, please don't tell anyone. I'll lose my job.'

'It can't be that bad,' I said. 'Fire away.'

Annie took a deep breath. 'It was on the Thursday. Ivy wasn't herself, as I told you. As I was going, she said, "You'd better have this now, pet. Don't open it till you get home. And don't tell anyone. Promise." I didn't tell anyone. The agency doesn't like us accepting gifts of money, but on my birthday or a Christmas, Ivy would always slip a tenner in with the card. Anyway, I slipped it in my bag. I thought, because it was bulky, she'd put a present in with the card and I thought maybe she didn't think she would last till Christmas, so I didn't open it. I thought, if there was a tenner in there, I'd need it more nearer to Christmas...' She paused to rummage in an inside pocket of her shoulder bag. 'Here it is,' she said, handing me the envelope. Inside was a Christmas card which read in a careful sloping hand – *For Annie, with grateful thanks. God bless and keep you. Love from Ivy. P.S. Don't forget to treat yourself.* Inside the card was £500.

'Wow,' I said. Then, as an afterthought, added, 'But at least if she had that sort of cash, robbery doesn't seem to be have been the motive.'

As soon as the words had left my mouth I regretted them. After all, which was worse – rape and robbery, or rape without additional motive? For some inexplicable reason, I thought rape alone was worst.

I left the warmth of Annie's home as a cold wind swept through the nearby trees. I shivered as I walked the few steps to my car. It was growing dark and I wanted to be home.

On the short journey back to Humberstone's, I couldn't help but notice the men I passed. Men in sombre clothes walking purposefully. Tall schoolboys going home from school laden with backpacks full of books. And the odd lone man walking, eyes down and jacket collar up. Suddenly, it seemed they were all suspects.

Three

Two days later, when I guessed the forensics team would be finished, I decided to visit Ivy's house. It was a cold and frosty morning, but the sun shone weakly, and with the daylight and a few encouraging words from Hubert about improved detection methods and his opinion that the Longborough police were as efficient as anywhere, I tried to stay positive.

I drove to Ivy's house. It was no longer enclosed by police ribbon, but a For Sale board was in place, which I thought, although somewhat hasty, was helpful because I could look like a prospective buyer. If I had been a viewer, I wouldn't have contemplated buying. It was a detached house with a plaque saying it was built in 1860. The window frames were rotten, the garden filled with weeds and the front door was painted a muddy brown. Ironically it was called Ivy Cottage, although the only ivy had been Ivy herself.

The front gate was half off its hinges but I

opened it carefully and looked around for watching eyes. To the right, next door's equally old house was neat and freshly painted, but there was no sign of life inside. On the left was a wide pathway and then the high fences of a primary-school playground.

There were two flowerpots amongst the weeds. I lifted them, feeling slightly guilty, as though I was trying to steal them – made worse by the fact that I also had the feeling I was being watched. There was no key under them.

I toyed with the idea of looking through the windows, but that would achieve nothing. I was closing the front gate when an old man carrying a plastic bag full of shopping seemed to appear from nowhere. He wore a cap, scarf and gloves, and he smiled, showing empty lower gums. 'I shouldn't buy that place if I were you, love. Gawd knows what went on there. I reckon she was murdered. The police have been in and out as often as a blacksmith's 'ammer goes up and down.'

'Did you know her?'

'Oh yes. Ivy and 'er 'usband lived round here for years. I live in the next road. It's quite posh 'ere really. Always been quiet, even with the school.'

I wasn't quite sure what to say next, but he was obviously in the mood to chat. 'So, what did you think of the inside?' he asked.

'I haven't seen it yet.'

'Well – last time I went in, it wasn't up to much. Old couple, too old to do improvements.'

'You visited, then?'

'Used to when the old man was there. But Ivy took to her bed most of the time, and it didn't seem right, if you know what I mean.' Then he added, 'If you want to look round, I could show you.'

He looked respectable enough but I hesitated. I really didn't think the police would have missed anything important, but I was torn between having a look round and wondering if I'd be wasting my time.

'You've got a key?' I asked.

'I've had one for years, love. I used to mow their back garden for them. Too much for them. Too much for me now.'

'Why did you need a key?'

'In case they were out,' he said. 'They kept the back gate bolted, so I had to go through the front if they were out. Mind you, it was only for hospital appointments or funerals. They didn't go out often.'

'Do the police know you've got a key?'

He looked puzzled. 'Should I tell them? I know Ivy kept a spare key under the flowerpot. I told her it was daft to do that, but she said it was in case of emergencies.'

'I think you should hand it in,' I said.

His bushy eyebrows closed together as he frowned. 'You're right. After all, I'm not a suspect.'

He waved cheerily as he walked away. In one way it was a result. But in another way it was ... odd. Had he been watching me? Where exactly had he sprung from? He had shopping with him but I hadn't seen a corner shop.

In my car, I rummaged around to find a mint, and sat for a few minutes sucking, crunching and thinking. If a dentally disadvantaged pensioner caused me even temporary suspicion, then I was getting paranoid. I supposed that if I'd been on a proper investigation, such a useful coincidence would never have happened.

I rang Annie to tell her that I hadn't found a key, but that a neighbour had one. 'Who was that then?' she asked. I swallowed hard. 'I didn't catch his name,' I said feebly. 'But he was old and partially toothless.'

'It could have been Fred Miles,' she said. 'Ivy mentioned him once or twice.'

Back at Humberstone's, Hubert was still out, and it wasn't long before Jasper gyrated dementedly around me demanding a walk. He was a good excuse to walk along Chorley Avenue. Although why I should want to, I didn't know. Just being nosy, I suppose.

Chorley Avenue consisted of semi-detached houses built in the seventies. The lawns and gardens had been tended with loving care in the summer, but now the flowers had sagged and faded.

It was easy to spot the murder house, it was taped off and two uniformed constables stood by the front door chatting. I walked past on the other side and glimpsed the garden shed. The door was ajar and I could see the forensics team moving about in white boiler suits like surgeons in some makeshift operating theatre.

I wondered if the murdered girl had heard her attacker come up behind her. Old Fred Miles had managed to creep up on me. I didn't know her name but tomorrow's newspapers would have all the details.

Feeling depressed at the upsurge in violence so close to home, I bent to stroke Jasper and felt thankful that dogs like him existed. Never petty or violent, Jasper merely wanted to please and be fussed.

I walked on briskly, allowing Jasper to think he was doing the pacing. I wanted to get home now. Somewhere very nearby was a murderer. Someone you passed in the street or smiled at in a shop as they served you. Any man, but not anywhere, for it seemed he was local. I hurried on as the daylight began to fade, and was grateful to see that Hubert's upper floor was lit like a beacon.

Hubert was in sombre mood and hardly commented when I told him I'd walked Jasper along Chorley Avenue. He simply carried on stirring a Bolognaise sauce as if, in its rich and murky depths, it would give him an answer. I sat nibbling a breadstick and sipping at a glass of yesterday's wine. It tasted sour and rough on the back of my throat.

At six p.m. Hubert switched on the TV in the kitchen for the news. The murder of eighteen-year-old Zoe Burrows was mentioned only in the regional news. A girl with dark tumbling hair, big brown eyes and a wide smiling face stared at us. A family friend spoke of her cheerful nature; her love of life, her physical fitness and how she'd been encouraged to take self-defence classes.

When it was over, Hubert switched off the TV and poured himself a large brandy.

'What's wrong?' I asked. 'Is it something I've done?'

He flashed me a wry smile. 'Not this time. The last funeral, it was ... worrying.'

'In what way?'

Hubert took another swig of brandy. 'It was the funeral of an elderly man. A Sidney Trees. His wife wanted to see him one last time this morning. Anyway, the poor old dear broke down completely, sobbing that she was glad he hadn't known what had happened to her.'

I didn't say anything. Funerals upset Hubert only occasionally. After all, it was his chosen profession, and usually it was the deaths of children and babies that saddened him. This was different.

'I sat her down,' he continued, 'and she told me all about it. Sidney had been in hospital for three weeks before he died. Every day she visited him and returned home in the evening about six. It happened one night in the second week. She'd gone to bed, taken a sleeping tablet, and hadn't heard a thing. What woke her she didn't know. But she opened her eyes to see the shape of a man in her room. He was just a black shape with eyes – wearing a balaclava.' Hubert paused. 'And then he raped her.'

I took a sip of Hubert's brandy, glad of the fire in my stomach. 'Why didn't she report it?'

'Because of Sidney, of course. If he'd heard about it, she knew it would kill him. In the event, he died anyway. She told me it was the only time she'd kept a secret from him.'

'But she'll report it now?'

Hubert shook his head. 'She's refusing to do that. And now she's too scared to stay in her own home and wants to go into residential care. At the moment there are no places, so she's stuck and she's terrified.'

'Did he steal anything?'

'Nothing. But he did say he'd be seeing her again.'

'She needs some police protection ... she needs...'

Hubert put up a hand to interrupt me. 'She needs someone like you to persuade her to talk to the police rape specialist.'

'You told me not to get involved.'

'This is as a friend. I told her you were an ex-nurse and that you worked for me.'

'Well, thanks for that. I'm not sure I'm up to it.'

'Of course you are. Look how well you coped with Ivy.'

'Ivy was dead. She could hardly cause me not to cope.'

Although I quibbled for a little longer, I knew I would see her. Now, with two rapes and a murder, surely that meant there was a maniac at large, and I would never have forgiven myself if I hadn't done something.

'When do you want me to go?'

He smiled in triumph. 'Today. She's emotional about the funeral, but she's talking. Leave it any longer and she might clam up.'

'Has she told anyone else?'

'She says not.'

'Won't she have dozens of people around her? Friends and relatives?'

40

'She's got a son but he left straight after the funeral. It seems his wife is very ill.'

'Will she let me in?'

'I'll ring her and let her know you're on your way. If she's got friends there, she'll think of an excuse.'

'I'll tell her I'm a social worker.'

'You could pass as one.'

'Thanks.'

As I left in the cold and dark, Hubert walked me to my car and was full of dire warnings. He'd pressed a spray he used to water his plants with into my hand, saying, 'If you should meet trouble, tell him it's acid. The power of suggestion can be a strong deterrent.'

'A sawn-off shotgun would be even more suggestive.'

'I'll ring you later,' he said, patting me on the back. 'Just to make sure you're OK.'

Mrs Alvira Trees lived on the Churchill estate, which consisted only of expensive bungalows. It was known locally as Wrinklies Hollow, because no one under sixty or so lived there. The estate was well lit and I saw that most of the bungalows had burglar alarms, but even so, it remained vulnerable, as some of the properties backed on to a large park often used by a few tearaway teenagers as a base for planning their various misdemeanours. Or at least that was the way

41

the local paper reported it.

Number 10, Winston Way, a cul-de-sac, proved hard to find, but eventually I found it, partly because three cars were parked on the front drive and a couple dressed in black were just leaving. I rang the doorbell and it was immediately opened by a middle-aged woman wearing a black and white suit and carrying a fur coat. 'You must be Kate,' she said. 'We're all just leaving. Now, I've told Alvira she only has to pick up the phone. We live over the road and she's more than welcome to stay with us, but it seems she wants to be on her own. She wants time on her own to think about Sidney – poor Sidney.' She smiled at me briefly, slipped on her fur coat, checked in the hall mirror that her grey perm was still in place, and then called out, 'Tom. Are you ready? There's a social worker here to see Alvira.' Tom appeared, followed by another more elderly couple. They smiled at me nervously. 'You go through to the lounge,' said Mrs Fur Coat. 'Alvira's expecting you. She's sitting down. It's too cold for her to hang round at the front door.'

As I walked down the short hallway and heard the click of the door closing, I felt a sense of relief that they'd gone. Years ago I'd had my share of a post-funeral gathering when my friends resolutely chose not to speak of my loss or of my partner. I only broke down when they'd gone, and I could hear as I opened the lounge door that Alvira too had waited. She sat hunched over on a three-seater sofa looking very alone. She was slim, wearing a black dress with a gold butterfly brooch on her right shoulder. Her grey hair was worn in a French pleat that was beginning to come apart. Her face in the glow of the coals of a gas fire looked pale and grey but her skin seemed unlined, and when she looked up, her eyes were filled with tears. 'You have a good cry if you want,' I said. 'Shall I make some tea?' She nodded and I left the room. On the kitchen table were the wrapped remains of the funeral tea. I couldn't hear her sobbing from the kitchen, but I sensed that she was. I took my time over the tea, and when I returned to the lounge, Alvira was hugging a box of tissues, a little breathless, but she was composed. She pointed to the coffee table and I placed the tray of tea down and sat beside her. She took my hand and held it tightly. 'What am I going to do?' she asked bleakly.

'About what?' I asked.

'About everything.'

'You mean being attacked or losing Sidney?

'Both.'

'Is there anything you *have* to do at the

moment?'

'No. Not now the funeral is over.'

'Good. All you need to do at the moment is grieve for him ... and yourself.'

'I'm so glad I didn't tell him,' she said. I sensed she wanted me to confirm that she did indeed do the right thing. So I smiled. 'It would have distressed him,' I said.

She nodded sadly. 'Mr Humberstone knows, and you know, but you're strangers. If I tell the police, and *if* he was caught, I'd have to testify, and then everyone would know and they'd be sorry for me twice over.'

I didn't say anything but I did pour the tea and handed her a cup. Her hand trembled and the bone-china cup rattled on the saucer. Gently I took the saucer away and put both her hands around the cup. We drank in silence. Alvira was in her seventies, comfortably off, living a quiet, respectable life in an attractive area, so who could blame her for not wanting her friends and neighbours to know. I too would want to avoid pitying glances and those who chose to ignore me because they didn't know what to say.

'You see,' she continued. 'I haven't got the courage. I know he has to be caught, but as I didn't report it at the time, it's too late now, and what difference will it make? That poor girl who was murdered – was she raped too?

Was it the same man?'

'I don't know. Maybe.'

Alvira stared at me for a moment. 'You think I should tell the police, don't you?'

'It's not a choice I'd want to make,' I said. 'And I think if my husband had just died, I would want to hide away for a while. You need to think only about yourself at the moment.'

'Thank you, dear,' she said. 'My mind is a bit of a blank. I can't even remember the funeral and that was a few hours ago.'

'You're in shock. Your memory will come back.'

'Some memories I don't want to come back.'

'About that night?'

She looked at me wearily, her eyes pools of misery. 'Yes. I was asleep. Something must have woken me. I remember calling out "Sidney – is that you?" I'd forgotten for a moment that he was in hospital...' She stopped and gulped, as if struggling for breath.

'Take your time,' I murmured. 'There's no rush.'

She stared at the bright artificial flames of the gas fire. 'I should have had a dog. A dog would have warned me. Sidney didn't want a dog. He said a pet was a tie and their hairs went everywhere. Just an excuse really...' She tailed off, deep in thought. 'He was a difficult man at times. Always thought he was right. But he was good to me. We had nothing when we first got married, but he worked at two jobs and we improved ourselves. He put in the burglar alarm system – it never worked, but he said the box was still a deterrent. He was wrong about that.'

Now her voice was weakening and she closed her eyes and leant back. 'Slip your shoes off,' I said. She slipped her shoes off and sighed. Very quietly, I continued to prompt her. 'You heard something and you thought it was Sidney?'

'Yes. Then it went quiet and I was drifting back to sleep when for some reason I opened my eyes. He was standing there. All in black. Just his eyes showing. I tried to switch on the bedside lamp but I knocked it to the floor in panic. He stood over me. He didn't say anything ... no, that's not true ... he did say something. He said my name ... *"Alvira."* He knew me.'

Four

Alvira began to sob again, only this time it seemed to me that fear was the trigger. I'd noticed there were various drinks in the kitchen. I took back the tea tray, found glasses and brandy and poured us both one, large ones.

She took the glass from me and gulped eagerly. Then she dabbed at her eyes with a tissue and took a deep breath.

'Did you recognize his voice?' I asked.

She shook her head and she put down the brandy glass as her hands began to tremble. 'I know how he got in,' she said. 'I didn't know then – not at first. I keep my keys on that little table in the hall – did you notice it?' I hadn't, in the to-ing and fro-ing of the funeral guests. 'I always kept my set of keys there,' she said. 'I think that somehow he managed to hook them through the letter-box. And then he let himself in.'

'What makes you think that?' I asked.

'When I was sure he'd gone, I rushed to the front door. He'd thrown the keys on the floor.'

I went to the hallway to look for myself. Sure enough, in the small hallway it would have been possible to hook a set of keys from the hall table. Once, when I'd been locked out, I'd done the same thing myself using a coat hanger.

'So that's how he got in,' I said.

'It doesn't explain how he knew my name,' murmured Alvira miserably.

'No,' I agreed. 'It doesn't.' At that moment I wasn't sure if it was the right time to ask her anything more about the actual rape. So I sipped my brandy and waited.

By now she'd finished her drink, but she still held the empty glass and was lost in her own thoughts or fears. 'I don't want to stay here on my own,' she said suddenly. 'But I don't feel ready for a home. I'm fit and active and I love my bungalow and my neighbours...' She broke off, choked with emotion.

'Why don't you stay with a friend for a few nights?'

She shook her head. 'They're couples. I'd feel in the way. These bungalows are fine for two but not three.'

'If I could find you somewhere to stay, would you consider that? You mentioned a dog – a few days away and you could get a dog and bring him back here. You wouldn't be alone then, and even a small dog can deter a hardened criminal.'

'I would like a dog,' she said, not sounding totally convinced.

She stared ahead blankly and after a few moments I said, 'I have a house in Farley Wood. A friend of mine lives there with her toddler. She likes company. I could ask her. If you can stand the thought of that.'

'You're very kind,' she said tearfully. 'But I don't want to be a nuisance.'

'You'll be a help. Megan and Katy will keep you busy.'

I rang Megan straight away, before Alvira could change her mind. As I expected, Megan asked no questions and said she'd be delighted to have some company, especially as my former nearly boyfriend DI David Todman was away on a course.

I put my mobile phone back in my shoulder bag. 'That's settled then,' I said. 'She's expecting us.' Panic swept across Alvira's face. 'What shall I take? What about telling people? What about my car?'

'Give me their telephone numbers,' I said. 'I'll ring them. Everything will be fine. Just pack a small bag.'

An hour later we arrived in Farley Wood. Megan opened the door with Katy in her arms, and Katy smiled at me instantly, but reserved a deeply puzzled frown for Alvira. Until, that is, Alvira patted her cheek and said softly, 'You're beautiful, aren't you, my darling.' Katy, being a woman in the making, loved flattery, and her chubby face became wreathed in smiles. For the first time since I'd met her, Alvira's face relaxed and she smiled back.

With Alvira in the living room with Katy, I made a pretence of helping Megan in the kitchen. Megan had blossomed since being reunited with Katy, and I guessed she was in love with David, although it was not only the love light in her eyes when his name was mentioned that made me think that. When I'd first met her, she'd been deeply traumatized, her baby taken from her. Then she'd been timid and frightened, wore shapeless cardies and flat shoes – now she was happy and confident, wore skimpy tops and make-up – and looked years younger. And yes, I was jealous.

'Are you sure you can manage this?' I asked.

'It'll be a pleasure,' she said in her soft lilting Welsh accent. 'I miss having your mother around.'

I didn't, but I made no comment. Megan would have seen the best in Saddam Hussein.

'Alvira's been recently widowed,' I explained, 'and she was attacked in her own home.'

50

'The poor soul,' said Megan as she paused from buttering bread.

'I think if she has a dog, she'll begin to feel safer once she goes home.'

'I'll help her choose one if that's what you want.'

'Thanks, Megan.'

We were about to return to the living room laden with sandwiches and tea and cake when I remembered to tell her that the 'attack' hadn't been reported to the police. It wasn't that I thought Megan would be indiscreet, but if David started asking questions, Megan would tell the truth. She looked at me and smiled. 'I'm not as naïve as I once was, Kate. I know how she feels. And if she wants to talk, I'll listen.'

I left it at that, and by the time I decided to go back to Humberstone's, it was growing dark. But the day had been worth it. Megan and I had done our good deeds and Alvira had won Katy's heart by playing on the floor with her. And I knew that with Megan's calm personality and gentle ways, Alvira might find a little peace.

As I drove away, I wondered what I would have done in the same circumstances and at the same age. Would I have rung the police and told them I'd been raped, or would I have jumped in a shower, ripped the sheets from the bed and burnt them, and then drunk a vast quantity of alcohol? I guessed the latter. It was easy to know the 'right' thing to do, but not so easy to do it.

I hoped Hubert wouldn't give me a hard time because I hadn't got more information. I wasn't, after all, on a 'job'. Alvira had chosen her path and that was going to be the end of it.

For the next few days I was conscious that Hubert was watching my every move. He tutted if he saw me watching daytime TV, and when I asked him what he thought I should be doing, he muttered about a bit of light housework wouldn't go amiss.

'Light housework,' I told him, 'does not exist.'

'Not in your world of indolence it doesn't,' he retorted.

'I repeat, Hubert,' I said frostily. 'What am I supposed to do? If my phone is always ringing, then I must be going deaf, because I don't hear it ring. And if, on the rare occasions it does ring, it's usually a crackpot.'

'That's your line of work,' he said.

'I can't take on just any old investigation.'

'Why not, if it pays?'

'There is often a moral issue to be considered,' I said.

I regretted those words as soon as they were out.

52

'Miss Hoity-Toity!' said Hubert. 'You're not in a convent or planning to take the cloth. I can't see that taking on a few cases of dog-napping or marital infidelity would make you lose your place in the queue for the pearly gates.'

Put like that, I didn't have much of an answer. And anyway, before I could come up with a suitable retort, Hubert had launched into a short diatribe about me underestimating the trauma of small losses. And why wasn't I spending more time with Megan and Mrs Trees?

'Because,' I snapped, 'Alvira needs peace and quiet, not me harassing her about the rape.'

'You don't do harassment,' he said. 'But you're good at finding excuses to do sod all.'

I took a deep breath, raised myself to my full height, gave him a rude sign and spent the rest of the day playing games on my computer. The phone didn't ring all afternoon, so by six p.m. I'd closed down my computer and felt vindicated in that I hadn't turned any work away.

At seven p.m. I was showered and had put on jogging bottoms and tee shirt to signal to Hubert that I was now relaxing after a hard day with my computer. I lay on the sofa to watch Channel Four News. Hubert was asleep in his brand-new recliner chair with

Jasper on his lap when I heard the wail of police sirens. The first time, I took little notice but it carried on, followed by the sound of an ambulance siren. I walked to the window. It was a clear frosty night, the moon was full and all the activity seemed to be based in the High Street. I could see the flashing lights and half expected to see smoke or fire engines. I stood for a moment just looking. Then I glanced at Hubert, whose open mouth had begun emitting hog-like snores, and a walk to the High Street seemed like respite.

I slipped on a coat, scarf and gloves and lifted Jasper gently from Hubert's arms. Hubert thankfully didn't stir. His mouth remained open like a dying fish gulping for air. A virus, codenamed by the medical profession 'There's a lot of it about', meant that the death toll amongst the frail elderly was rising. I reasoned that, with Hubert in the deep sleep of the hardworking and righteous, I could be out and back before he even missed me.

In the High Street, although I had the excuse of walking Jasper, I was still one of many nosey parkers eager to find out what had happened.

One of the alleyways by the side of the new McDonald's had been cordoned off, uniformed police were everywhere and 'passersby' were trying to find out what had happened. In amongst the throng, I couldn't fail to notice DCI 'Twice' Waterworth. And he didn't fail to notice me. In fact he began to walk towards me. I didn't want to speak to him, so I backed away hoping he'd get the message. Instead he came up close and breathed garlic at me. 'How come you've heard so soon?' he muttered. I did wonder if ill-fitting dentures affected his speech, but that hardly mattered because I didn't know what he was talking about. 'What do you mean? I heard the sirens.' He looked at me warily. 'You know who the victim is?' he asked.

'No. How would I know?'

'It's Alice...'

I didn't give him a chance to finish. 'Alice who?'

'Alice ... Dawes,' he said, enunciating as if speaking to a deaf person.

'Alice from Humberstone's?' I queried.

'That's the one.'

'She's not...'

'I'm afraid so. Very dead.'

If Jasper hadn't yanked his lead at that point, I think I would have been sick. I'd only met Alice about twice. She did the make-up and the flowers. A cheerful woman in her fifties, barely five feet tall. I finally found my voice. 'What was she doing here?'

'It seems she'd been to see her GP in the High Street. I reckon she was dragged into the alleyway as she passed by.'

'How was she killed?'

'Strangled.'

'Was she raped?'

'No idea yet. Didn't look like it.'

As I walked away, Waterworth called after me. 'We'll get him. We'll get him.'

I dreaded telling Hubert. The walk back was slow, Jasper wanted to sniff every doorpost and tree, and it gave me time to worry about Hubert's reaction. His staff was his family, he chose them carefully and he was a loyal caring boss. I kept my distance, not wanting to be drawn into the day-to-day running of the business. I felt I couldn't do two jobs. Being a struggling PI was as much as I could cope with. Now for some reason I felt guilty, as though, as the messenger, I was in some way to blame.

Hubert began to stir as we walked into the room. He opened one eye, 'Have I been snoring?'

'I don't know. I've been out with Jasper.'

'You shouldn't go out on your own. I would have come with you.'

'I know. I went out because I saw police and an ambulance in the High Street.'

'What was it?'

'It's bad news ... it's someone you know.'

56

Anxiety flickered in his eyes. 'Who?'

'Alice. I'm so sorry.'

Hubert's hands shook and he clenched his lips together. 'What happened?' he asked after a few moments.

'She'd been to see her doctor. She was walking past that alleyway by McDonald's, and it seems he grabbed her and strangled her.'

I could see he was struggling for words, so I put my arm around him.

'Bastard ... the evil murdering bastard,' he murmured. 'I can't believe it. She was a lovely little woman.' He paused to look at me hopefully. 'Are you sure it was our Alice?'

I nodded and poured him a brandy. He drank it quickly. 'What's happening?' he asked. 'What the hell is going on?'

There was of course no answer. Or none that we knew. Hubert sat glumly for several minutes. Then he stood up, straightened his shoulders and said, 'I've things to do. I'm going to call a meeting of all the staff. I'd appreciate it if you'd come, Kate.'

'Yes, of course. When do you want the meeting?'

'Tonight. As soon as everyone can get here.'

At the door, he turned. 'This is it, Kate. You're involved now. And so am I. If the police can't get him – we will! This is

57

personal, and when I find him ... I'll kill him.'

I'd never heard Hubert say anything like that before. It shocked me. And made me more aware than ever that, somehow, our cosy little world, if you could call a funeral business cosy, was in danger of being destroyed.

Five

The meeting began at nine p.m. in the catering suite. Temporary and permanent staff were present, and it was obvious from Hubert's grim expression that some very serious news was about to be imparted. I sat with Joy at a table for two at the back of the room.

'Hubert's not retiring, is he?' she asked. I shook my head. She looked around the room. 'I thought Alice would be here,' she said. 'She was being signed off by her doctor.'

'Could I have your attention please,' Hubert boomed above the loud murmuring. 'I have some tragic news to impart.' There was total silence as he told them Alice had been murdered. Even when he'd finished talking, the silence continued for a few minutes. Then, as shock gave way to realization, Joy and the catering manager, Pam, could be heard sobbing. I noticed one or two of the drivers teary-eyed and sniffing. Hubert's final words were, 'Everyone must be vigilant – especially women. This man is a maniac and we all need to keep our eyes and ears open, especially if we see anyone behaving suspiciously.'

I sat with my arm around Joy and provided tissues. 'She lived alone,' she said sniffing. 'A little terraced house. She never married. Who could have wanted to kill her?' There was no answer to that, so I kept quiet. 'How was she killed?' asked Joy.

'Strangled.'

Joy gave a huge sigh. 'Poor Alice. She did have a man friend, you know.'

I didn't.

'I met him once – Harry,' she continued with another sigh. 'Nice bloke. He'll be devastated. He wanted to marry her for years, but she kept saying no. She had lots of friends – she was a lovely person...' As she broke off, we could hear the change in the room. Angry voices were raised and certain words seemed to hang in the air – 'newcomer', 'stranger' and then finally 'asylum seeker'.

In Longborough of recent months, a few asylum seekers had been housed in one of the least desirable council estates. Mostly young men, they were recognizable by their mock-leather jackets and worried expressions. They had been so little trouble they were practically invisible, but no doubt the local police had been keeping an eye on them.

Hubert heard the circulating rumours and suggested no one was beyond suspicion, and that the police would soon start interviewing them. A thoughtful silence then descended, and it wasn't long before the now sombre staff made their way home.

It was growing late, but Hubert wanted to discuss our strategy for catching the murderer. I would have preferred him not to be involved, because he was still so emotional. I'd hardly known Alice, so I was sorry but not as upset as Hubert.

In the kitchen, we drank cocoa, as Hubert seemed to think we needed a clear head. Personally, one or two alcoholic drinks usually spark my optimism; Hubert needed no such trigger. He was convinced we'd crack the case in a couple of weeks.

'We can do nothing,' I said, 'without police help.'

He looked about to disagree, but then said, 'David Todman's back.'

'Megan didn't say.'

'Well, he is.'

I felt a bit peeved that Megan hadn't thought to mention his return. She'd mentioned on the phone that Alvira had her sights on a Westie and that she wanted to see me. I hoped that was because she had remembered something. David had not been mentioned at all.

'I think you should ring him first thing in the morning,' said Hubert. 'Use all your womanly charms.'

'I think I'd have more luck with Twice Waterworth.'

'Why do you call him "Twice"?'

'He mumbles and often says things twice.'

'Married?'

'I expect so,' I said. 'To some poor forlorn soul. He looks just like Hitler.'

'I heard Hitler was attractive to women.'

'That was power, not his looks.'

'We're going off the point, Kate. Ring David and ask him what's going on. Have they got any suspects?'

'I wouldn't have thought so,' I said sharply. 'After all, how many enemies could a woman like Alice have had?'

'That's true,' he conceded. 'It sounds like a random killing.'

I thought about that for a few moments. Murder with a motive, be it money, sex, jealousy, was not too difficult to understand. But to kill a complete stranger simply hauled off the road was incomprehensible unless it was drug or drink-fuelled – or a case of mistaken identity. But, until we knew more about the cause of death, mere speculation wasn't going to help.

I promised Hubert I'd ring David in the morning and bribe him with a pub lunch and hopefully he'd reward me with snippets of information.

'Ring him now,' he said, 'and arrange it, and then I can go to bed happy.'

Reluctantly I agreed and went up to my office to make the call. I didn't want Hubert hearing David turn me down. Luckily he didn't. 'Yeah, why not, Kate. It'll make a change from all the bullshit I've been listening to at Bramshill.'

'How's Megan?' I asked. I was, of course, merely fishing.

'You know she's fine,' he said. 'I've been playing gooseberry with the old lady. Your idea, I believe?'

'Yes. One of my better ones, I thought.'

'Not from my point of view. What exactly is wrong with her?'

'Her husband died very recently and, whilst he was in hospital, she was raped in her own home.'

He paused and sighed. 'Fair enough. Has she reported it?'

'No. Too ashamed.'

'We'll talk about that as well.'

'As well as?'

'Don't play the innocent. I'll see you at the Crown – twelve thirty p.m.'

Was it my imagination or had David

changed? His attitude seemed more determined. Perhaps his course had been on assertiveness, or was he lined up for promotion and he was practising his role. Either way, he seemed different.

Next day I was a little late arriving at the Crown. David sat in a corner seat nursing a pint of beer. He didn't usually drink in the middle of the day, and he'd obviously walked from the police station, because he wouldn't ever drink and drive. But the way he sat with his head down, staring into his pint glass engrossed in thought, suggested that he was depressed. He smiled and stood up when he saw me. 'You're looking good,' he said.

'I can scrub up quite well – if I make the effort.'

He went to the bar to order the drinks and the meals. I offered him the money but he refused. 'No way. I'm paying,' he said. 'I need a sounding board.'

Strangely I was flattered. Me! A sounding board for a policeman.

He came back with a glass of red wine for me and another pint for himself. I knew that something was wrong. 'Trouble at mill?' I queried.

'Yeah. Is it that obvious?'

He sat silently sipping his beer until I was forced to say something. 'How was the course?'

'Political claptrap,' he snapped back. 'It's no wonder criminals are having a field day. The police force now is so concerned with the rights of its officers and protecting them from prejudice or physical harm, soon we'll be patrolling the streets in groups of six wearing riot gear.'

'I wish I hadn't asked,' I said lightly.

He managed a wry smile. After a short pause, he said, 'I heard about Alice. I met her once. I really liked her. I suppose you're angling for information, and it's not my body you're after?'

'Perceptive as ever,' I said, smiling, still trying to lighten his mood.

'I suppose you want to know how Alice died and if we have any leads?'

I nodded.

'Poor Alice was manually strangled after being punched several times in the face. The pathologist thinks the first blows might have rendered her unconscious.'

'I hope so,' I murmured.

'Not much consolation to her friend Harry. He's in a terrible state and he doesn't know the half of it yet.'

'What's that supposed to mean?'

He shrugged but looked reluctant to say more. And I began to allow two and two to make four. 'You probably know,' I said, 'that Ivy Waites was raped, and of course Alvira. I

65

just wondered how many more old ladies have been raped and not reported it.'

He stared at me for a moment and looked about to speak. The sort of look a man has before telling you he's seeing another woman or you're about to be dumped. A cross between shifty and anxious.

'I shouldn't be telling you this, and I'm only telling you now because Waterworth is such an incompetent...' He paused. 'You've met him, you know what I mean.'

I waited. It seemed he was going to tell me something important. And he was.

'The PM showed some evidence that she had been raped a few days before. There were bruises on her wrists and legs. That was her "sickness". She admitted to her doctor she'd been raped. He tried to persuade her to report it but she refused. She didn't want Harry to know.'

'How did he get in?' I asked.

'He didn't break in. It seems she woke up and he was in her bedroom.'

'All dressed in black and calling her by name.'

David looked surprised. 'How the hell did you know that?'

'That's what Alvira told me. It makes me think the rapist did know Alvira.'

David drained his first pint and started his second. 'It's unusual,' he muttered. 'But what do you think it means?'

'With two murders and at least three rapes,' I said. 'It's an epidemic. I can't help thinking that if three older women didn't want to report their attack – how many others are there, and over what time span?'

'Mass rape of old ladies and two murders,' said David grimly, 'is enough to start panic in the streets.'

'There were murmurings at Humberstone's,' I said, 'about illegal immigrants – you know the sort of thing – strangers in our midst.'

'You can understand that,' he said. 'Longborough suddenly has murders and rapes where, before, a 'crime' was two teenagers smoking pot on a Saturday night, or the odd drunken brawl...'

He broke off as a silent-footed barmaid delivered our food to us. She'd obviously overheard us. Her name badge read, *Jade*, and she was about nineteen, with straight blonde hair and a whippet-thin body. 'You're cops, aren't you?' It was almost an accusation.

'Yeah, we're cops,' said David with a smile. 'Do we get a discount?'

'You'll be lucky,' she said. 'The boss would walk half a mile for one penny lying on the ground. I just want to tell you something. It's been worrying me.'

'Take your time,' said David. 'Sit down.'

She looked around slightly anxiously. 'I'd better not. I get my break in an hour. Will you still be here? It is important...' She broke off.

We watched her glide away, and then David muttered, 'I hope it's real information. Waterworth is concerned about progress as it is. He thinks we have a psycho on the loose, and when he catches him, he'll be the golden-balls of the Midlands police.'

'And what do you think?'

He thought for a moment. 'I've heard a whisper that the Chief Constable wants to bring in a psychological profiler. Waterworth will do all he can to stop that. He wants all the credit.'

'Do you think a profiler is a good idea?' I asked as I picked up my knife and fork, because the sight and smell of my plaice and chips had become overwhelming.

'I'd like to think Longborough police could manage on their own,' he said, picking up a chip. 'But I'm not convinced they can. This is one of those cases where we'll need all the help we can get.'

After a while, I said, 'The rapist isn't a stranger, or at least in Alice and Alvira's case, because he knew their names. What are the odds of there being more than one rapist and murderer in the area?'

David shrugged. 'No idea. Wouldn't like to hazard a guess.'

He continued eating. 'I'm warning you, Kate. If Waterworth finds out you're involved in investigating Alice's death – he's a hard bastard. He'll wreck your agency.'

'I'll have to be careful then,' I said. I tried to sound unconcerned, but I wasn't. If Waterworth thought his case might be jeopardized, then I had to keep a mouse-like profile. This would be hard, as I'd never managed it before.

We finished eating, David went for more drinks, and then we chatted about Katy and Megan for a while. 'So, it's serious then – you and Megan?' I asked.

He smiled. 'She's very self-sufficient. I'm a little extra in her life, but that's all. It's sad, but true.' He sipped his beer and that topic was at an end. I'd thought he and Megan were ideally suited, but obviously matchmaking wasn't one of my skills.

We chatted inconsequentially for a few more minutes, until Jade appeared and took a seat beside us. She still looked nervous – maybe it was talking to a police inspector, or perhaps it was something else. Either way, she was uncomfortable.

'It's about Zoe Burrows, the dead girl – I didn't know her very well, but we went to the same school. I was in the year above her.

Sometimes I saw her at a nightclub in Birmingham. I was sworn to secrecy, because if her Dad had found out, there would have been trouble. Then, about a month ago, I met her while I was out shopping. She looked a bit down in the dumps, so I suggested we went for a drink. It was then that she told me...' She broke off. 'She said she'd been attacked on her way home from the train station.'

She fell silent then, and David suggested she had a drink. She asked for a Diet Coke, and while he was at the bar, I said, 'You're doing the right thing in telling us.'

'Am I? I'm scared. I live alone and I often walk home alone. I don't think I can do it any more.'

David arrived with her Diet Coke before I had a chance to respond. 'Now then, Jade, you were saying that Zoe was attacked on her way home from the station.'

'Yeah. She knew she was being followed. So she hung back, pretending to use her mobile. When she turned round he was gone.'

'Did she get any sort of look at him?' asked David.

'No. She walked on fast but he was waiting for her on the next corner – hiding in the shadows. As she passed by, he called out her name. Then he attacked her from behind.

She raked her stiletto heels down his shin and he let go then – and she ran for it.'

'She must have seen him,' said David quietly. 'If he called her name, she would have turned around.'

'No. She said not. But she did say she recognized his voice.'

Six

We waited for Jade to say more. 'Why are you looking at me like that?' she asked.

'You did say Zoe recognized his voice,' said David quietly.

'Yeah. But she wouldn't tell me who. She hadn't seen his face. She only *thought* she recognized his voice.'

'OK,' said David, sounding a little tense. 'Why the hell didn't she report it?'

Jade sipped her Coca-Cola. 'I dunno, but I think it was because she was scared of her dad. She was always lying to him about where she was and who she was with.'

'She's eighteen,' I said, then corrected myself. 'She *was* eighteen. Not a kid any more.'

Jade nodded. 'But her dad's old-fashioned and religious. I never met him but I didn't like what I heard about him.'

'From Zoe?'

'Yeah. He sounded ... odd. I think he's a bit of a nutter.'

'And her mum?' I asked.

'She was OK. I think she knew what was

going on, but she didn't want to create ructions.'

'So, only her friends really knew Zoe?' I said.

'I suppose so,' said Jade thoughtfully. 'Although she didn't really have many friends. Her dad belongs to one of those weird churches and he only approved of one or two of her girlfriends.'

'Those that went to church?' asked David.

'Yeah.'

'And which church was that?'

'The Methodist church in the town.'

I tried to keep a straight face. I'd had visions of the Plymouth Brethren at the very least. David raised his eyebrows and flashed me a little smile.

'What have I said?' asked Jade sharply.

'It's just that the Methodist Church is middle of the road,' I answered. 'They don't like gambling but they're not exactly "weird".'

Jade shrugged. 'Have it your way. That's what Zoe told me. I don't go to church, so I wouldn't know. Didn't do Zoe much good, did it? Poor cow gets murdered.'

Jade stood up, her bottle of Coke half-drunk. 'I've told you all I know,' she snapped. 'You'd better catch him, 'cos I'm fed up of being scared.' Then she walked off, no longer gliding, but obviously in a shoulders-back, striding huff.

'Well, we didn't handle that well, did we?' said David as we watched her disappear behind the bar.

We sat for a while picking at the cool remains of our meals. 'I think,' said David slowly, 'we're undermanned for this one. We're checking the sex-offenders register – and that takes forever. And we're following up psychiatric patients on care-in-the-community orders. The DNA and forensics could take weeks. In the meantime, we're giving out warnings to women about not being out alone after dark and not opening their doors to strangers...'

'That's just the point, isn't it,' I interrupted. 'This man isn't necessarily a stranger.'

'There could be more than one,' suggested David.

'Is that likely?'

'There are theories around about collective madness.'

'You mean someone starts killing and, like a virus, it infects someone else?'

'It's only a theory, Kate.'

I wasn't sure what I thought any more. Alice, I told myself, was my only concern. Capitalizing on David's presence, I asked for Alice's boyfriend's address.

'Best place to find him is at Harry's Place. The sandwich bar just off the High Street. He's the owner. Just don't let Waterworth find out. And Kate – do me a favour.'

'What's that?'

'Don't go out alone after dark.'

Harry's Place supplied two tables for eating in, and boasted the fastest sandwich in the Midlands. The sandwich fillings were kept in plastic boxes in the chill cabinet and, along with numerous fillings, the 'sandwich' could be anything from plain white cut bread to tortilla wraps. There was a short queue and I stood in line and watched as the two assistants, one male, one female, deftly filled and wrapped.

The male sandwich-maker was, I guessed, in his late thirties, medium height, with receding dark hair. The female, perhaps forty, was short, with an ample bosom and flushed cheeks. Their customers were obviously regulars, because, as they dished out the fillings, the banter was friendly and personal. When it came to my turn, I already knew from the other customers it was Tone – I presumed for Tony. His partner was 'Sal'.

'What can I get you, sweetheart?' he asked.

'Nothing, thanks. I've come to see Harry.'

'Police?'

'No. I'm Kate from Humberstone's.'

He gave me a searching look. 'Hang on then, Kate. I'll see if he's up to it.'

He disappeared into a back room. Sal

served the only customer behind me, a middle-aged man in a grey pinstripe. His sandwich was quickly prepared and wrapped. He thanked her between tight lips, gave her the exact money and left. 'He's a funny bloke,' said Sal with a smile. 'Has the same thing every day – tuna mayonnaise on white sliced. Never varied it in a whole year. I reckon he thinks it's an aphrodisiac.'

It took me a moment to understand her slow phonetic pronunciation of the word.

'You come to see Harry then?' she asked as she covered the container of tuna and mayonnaise.

I nodded.

'He's in a bad way,' she said. 'He's not eating. He looks terrible. Blames himself of course.'

'There was nothing he could have done.'

'You try telling him that.'

A few moments later, 'Tone' reappeared, smiled and nodded his head in the direction of the back room.

I found Harry in a windowless room sitting at a table surrounded by packing boxes and shelves of tinned food and cleaning equipment. The single bulb overhead meant the light was poor and cast shadows on Harry's face. He was wearing a white shirt and black tie and had deep bags under his eyes. On the table were several invoices and a half-empty bottle of whisky. As he looked up, he brought a tumbler to his lips and gulped the remains of the glass. He pointed to the empty chair beside him and then poured himself another whisky. 'Only thing that helps,' he said. 'What can I do for you, Kate? Alice told me about you. She said ... you were some sort of private investigator.'

He was beginning to slur his words, but I smiled. If he was disinhibited, I might, just might, find out more. 'She was right,' I said. 'I am a PI, and Mr Humberstone wants me to investigate Alice's murder.'

'Think you're better than the police then?' He swigged heavily on the whisky.

'Not at all. But they are overstretched. We don't want Alice's murder to be overlooked.'

'Nor her rape ... If I get the bastard I'll kill him. Alice was my life. Kindness itself she was...' He broke off completely and stared at me. 'You're a woman ... why didn't she tell me? Why?'

I took a deep breath. His eyes were filling with tears and his voice was cracking up.

'She didn't want to distress you,' I said quietly. 'What you didn't know wouldn't hurt you.'

He continued to stare at me. 'I could have protected her. Been with her, looked out for her. Now she's dead because a rapist came back to ... to silence her.' His head slumped forward on to the table and I knew he was weeping, because his back moved, but there was no sound.

I stayed, patting his shoulder, and after a while he rested his head on his hands and fell asleep.

I left then, telling Tone and Sal that Harry had fallen asleep and could they keep an eye on him.

Outside, the cold air caught my breath and I hurried back to Humberstone's with my collar up, deep in thought. Harry had made the situation clear. It had been staring us in the face. The rapist and the murderer were one. He came back to silence his victim. Even though his victims had not reported the crime. Had he in fact warned them? Only Alvira would be able to tell me that. As long as I wasn't too late.

Seven

It was after six p.m. when Hubert came upstairs to the kitchen. As he stood in the doorway slipping off his black overcoat, I thought how old and careworn he looked. Jasper, tail wagging excitedly around his feet, was ignored. Hubert placed his overcoat over his arm, said, 'I'm perished,' and then disappeared for a few minutes.

When he returned, he was wearing a blue sweatshirt with matching trouser bottoms. I handed him a mug of tea and thought I detected a slight expression of disappointment that it wasn't something stronger. He sat down at the kitchen table, lifted Jasper on to his lap and sampled the tea. 'Did you see Harry?' he asked.

'Yep. I saw him.'

'And?' queried Hubert impatiently.

'He was very upset. In fact he was drunk.'

'So, you didn't find out anything?'

Suddenly I was irritated. 'I can't force information from a grieving man. In time he'll tell me more.'

'Maybe at this very minute the murderer has a victim in his sights,' said Hubert, somewhat overdramatically I thought, so I ignored the comment.

'Harry didn't know, until the police told him, that Alice had been raped – he's unlikely to be able to help much. Although...' I broke off. 'Well ... he did say something about the rapist coming back to silence her. That made me think Alvira may be withholding information, or she knows more than she realizes.'

'What are you waiting for?' said Hubert. 'Get out to Farley Wood and find out.'

I couldn't admit that I really didn't want to go out after dark. I told myself I was being a wimp. Life has to go on, and I had a car, so I really had no excuse. I rang Megan to say I was on my way. As I left, I said, 'If I'm not back in two hours, send out a search party.' Hubert, reading the paper, lowered his glasses. 'It's not a joke. Just be careful.'

I didn't feel one bit jocular as I made my way across the empty car park. It was cloudy, no sign of a moon, and chillingly damp. As I drove out of Longborough, the streets were deserted, the Christmas decorations and lights glowing sadly in the dark.

Farley Wood was equally deserted, but Megan had put lights up at the window, which did lift my spirits. The sight of a real but early Christmas tree, with only an angel on top, but boxes of baubles opened in readiness, also lifted my spirits. A glass of mulled wine helped even more.

Alvira had been reading a novel and it lay open on the arm of her chair. I had the feeling I was an unwelcome intrusion, a reminder of trauma that she would rather forget. When I asked about her plans over Christmas, she said, 'Megan's kindly asked me to stay over Christmas, so I'll be delighted to do that.' I should have anticipated it, but I hadn't, and now I felt disappointed. I had hoped Megan and Katy would come to Humberstone's. Hubert would have loved it. 'You and Hubert are very welcome to come here, Kate,' said Megan, sensing I felt a little left out.

'I can't leave Hubert on his own,' I said. 'He'll be on call. People die on Christmas Day, and there's just a driver on standby.'

Katy whimpered from upstairs, and Megan, attuned to her daughter's cry, rushed to her. I sat beside Alvira, and as I did so, she tensed slightly. 'I want to forget it ever happened,' she said. 'After Christmas, I'll go home with my dog and I'll try to get on with my life ... alone.'

I sat silently for a few moments. 'I do understand,' I said.

'No you don't,' she said sharply. 'You want

me to report it for the sake of others. I wish I could. I know that's the right thing to do. But at the moment I can only think about myself.'

'I am thinking of you,' I said. 'You see ... Alice from Humberstone's was raped a week before she was murdered. Her partner seems to think the rapist had to silence her.'

Alvira's face paled and her hands trembled. Then she took a deep breath and said, 'There you are then – she shouldn't have reported it. She'd still be alive if she'd kept quiet.'

'She didn't report it – not to the police at least. She told only her doctor. He tried to encourage her to go to the police but she refused. It seems she didn't want to upset her partner.'

Alvira's hand went to her mouth. Then, breaking into the silence, from upstairs we could hear Megan singing a Welsh lullaby to Katy. We listened intently to Megan's clear voice. Neither of us understood the words, but it didn't matter. It was about innocence and kindness and a mother soothing her child. It seemed to have an affect on Alvira.

'I can't go to the police, I just can't, but I'll answer any questions you ask me. I go over and over it in my mind. Sometimes I doubt my sanity – think I'm becoming senile.'

'You seem very sharp to me.'

'I left keys where it was easy for him to reach them.'

'You couldn't have known that.'

'No, but we've always been very careful – my husband is ... was ... very security-conscious. Every year, especially near Christmas, there were one or two burglaries, so we always checked the doors and windows last thing at night.'

'But no alarm system?'

She shook her head. 'No, we tried one once – it kept going off and no one took any notice. The box is still there as a deterrent.' She paused. 'It didn't work, though, did it?' she murmured.

'Tell me again,' I said, 'what you remember about that night.'

She gazed at me sadly then, as if realizing she had no option. In a wavering voice, she said, 'I had a bath about nine thirty and I was in bed by ten. I planned to read but I took a sleeping pill and I was so tired that I only managed a page of my book...'

'What woke you?'

'I don't know. I told you before ... I opened my eyes and there was a dark figure in the room. He ... he pulled back the duvet and then ... he raped me.' Alvira's voice, already weak, cracked, and she swallowed hard. She tried to speak again but no sound came.

'Don't try to speak any more,' I said,

feeling guilty that I'd reduced her to virtual jelly. 'Just answer yes or no if you can.'

She nodded with tear-filled eyes. 'Did he speak?'

'Yes,' she croaked.

'He called you by name?'

'Yes.'

'Did he threaten you?'

'Yes.'

'Did he say he would kill you if you reported the attack?'

There was a long pause – tears escaped down her cheeks. She looked grey with anxiety. 'Yes,' she whispered.

At that moment, Megan came into the room. She looked from Alvira to me, and for the first time since I'd known her, she looked tight-lipped and furious. 'How could you be so unkind, Kate? Alvira's suffered enough. Can't you just leave her alone? She's told you all she knows, and if she remembers something in the future, I'm sure she'll let you know.'

Megan sat down beside Alvira and stroked her hair while Alvira sobbed and I felt like the worst bitch in the world. I mumbled my apologies and left.

On the drive back, I too felt like crying. How the hell was I going to investigate Alice's death with one frightened elderly victim as the only witness? Hubert wouldn't be best pleased, but if he had any ideas about my next step, I'd be more than willing to listen.

When I did get back, I saw him watching from the kitchen window.

'I've been worried sick,' he said as he met me on the stairs. 'Where have you been?'

'You were the one who told me to get out to Farley Wood to see Alvira.'

'Oh yes. I remember now ... sorry, Kate. I'm a bit preoccupied.'

Once more I felt a little twinge of anxiety about Hubert. He was working too hard and Alice's death seemed to have affected his confidence. He made a pot of tea and asked how hungry I was. As usual, I was in I'll-eat-anything mode, as long as it's cooked for me. He suggested pork chops with a brandy, cream and mustard sauce, with potato croquettes and runner beans, which sounded jolly good. 'Home-made croquettes?' I ventured.

'Don't be bloody silly,' he said. Then, seeing the expression on my face, he began to laugh. And laugh. I joined in. I couldn't help it, but I didn't really know what was so funny. When he stopped laughing, he said, 'Don't you think making potato croquettes is a bit poncey?'

'It's not something that's ever crossed my mind,' I said. 'Are you sure you're all right,

Hubert? You seem a bit...'

'Flaky?'

'No, I wasn't going to say that.'

'But you were thinking it.'

'I was not!'

Hubert placed his mug of tea on the table. 'If you must know, I've been feeling guilty.'

'What about?'

'About Alice.'

'Why?'

He shrugged. 'I didn't take much notice of her. She went off sick and I didn't ring her to ask how she was. I should have gone to see her. She lived alone. If I had, she might have told me. She might still be alive...'

'I really don't think she would have told you. You have nothing to reproach yourself for.'

Hubert didn't look one bit reassured, so I tried a different tack. 'I'll need some input from you,' I said. 'I know you're busy, but I need a bit of guidance on what to do next.'

I was playing him like a violin, but he didn't seem to notice. 'You're right,' he said. 'We have to stay focused, it's no good looking back. We need a list. You start that, I'll start cooking.'

I reasoned there was incompetence and downright stupidity – not wanting to show the latter, I didn't ask what sort of list he wanted. I stared for a while at a blank sheet of paper while Hubert played chef and sipped at the cooking brandy.

I listed the victims. One thing was more than obvious, if the perpetrator was the same man and was murderously inclined towards older, even elderly, women, where did young Zoe fit in? What would a profiler say about the murderer? One, he was local. Two, he knew his victims. Probably he would be aged between twenty-five and forty-five. According to Alvira, he was tallish but not fat. He wore black with a black balaclava. Had there been any DNA evidence? A fibre from his clothes? Unless he'd had a previous conviction, DNA evidence was only part of the journey towards arresting a suspect. Obviously I'd be the last to know if the police did have a suspect.

My 'list' was a spidery mess, but as Hubert called out, 'Grubs up!' I wrote one sentence – *What do the victims have in common?*

As Hubert placed my meal in front of me, he said, 'Have you cracked it yet then?'

I didn't answer. The food smelt good, it looked good, and sometimes food has to come first.

Later, mellow with food and a little brandy, we tried to work out what Zoe, Ivy, Alvira and Alice could have in common. We checked out their addresses – all lived within a small circle. The postman and the milkman

87

were a possibility. 'You could check them out,' said Hubert.

'What do I say to them? Excuse me, are you a homicidal maniac? A loner with a balaclava in your milk crate or your post bag?'

'There's no need to take that attitude,' said Hubert, looking with slight disgust at my 'list'. 'We have to look at every possibility.'

I agreed and suggested doctors, dentists, plumbers, mechanics, carpet layers, estate agents, vicars – anyone who could have been male and have associated with our victims.

Hubert knitted his brows so deeply they could have formed a small scarf. 'Now you're going for overkill,' he said.

'I am not!'

'Yes you are.'

Our childishness ceased as the phone rang. Hubert answered it, listening intently for a minute or two, then he murmured, 'Oh no,' followed by, 'Yes, of course she'll come. About five minutes? Fine. Bye.'

He put the phone down slowly and looked across to me. 'You'd better get togged up for the great outdoors.'

'What's happened?'

'That was David. He needs a favour.'

I hesitated. Why not speak to me personally? I'd noted the 'she'll come'. I was deeply suspicious.

'There's been another old lady raped. And

she's reported it.'

'I'm sorry, but what does David want me to do?'

'He wants you to sit with her.' Then he added. 'Overnight. She's been to the police station – unfortunately, she left it for two days before reporting it.'

'So, there'll be no forensics?'

Hubert shrugged. 'David says they haven't got a WPC to spare and they are fully stretched, but they don't want to send her back to an empty house – she's refused to go to hospital.'

'She's injured?'

'Black eyes. A split lip and bruising. She put up a hell of a fight.'

I was already slipping on my boots. Hubert wrote down the address for me and collected my coat from the hall stand. Jasper, meanwhile, raised from torpor by the phone ringing, was chasing his tail with excitement. I looked at Hubert. 'Shall I take Jasper?'

'She may not like dogs.'

When I pointed to his bed, Jasper slunk away disappointed.

I checked the name and address. Betty Scott, 4 Station Road. I knew where it was, barely half a mile away, a side road that led from the station, the houses built in the 1890s to house the railway workers.

As I walked outside, the rawness of the

cold air hit me. Frost was already forming and the moon was full. Hubert stood by my car and waited until I started the engine. 'Take care,' he said. 'Just stay on your guard.'

I didn't answer. After all, I was only going to sit with an old lady with the guts to report that she'd been raped.

Eight

Station Road, where Betty lived, was a narrow street of terraced houses that had become a most desirable place to live. The two-up two-down dwellings had been extended with attic rooms and conservatories at the back. From there, commuters to London and Birmingham could walk to the station and walk home again if there were major train delays. Consequently they were expensive and bought mainly by singles or childless couples who planned to stay only until they found somewhere better. On my walks with Jasper, I had seen a few interiors. Walls had been knocked down and French windows added. They seemed clutter-free, with lighting that exhibited their most precious possessions. More museum than home. One or two remained oblivious to suggestions made by television stylists. Those were, I guessed, the pensioners who couldn't afford or didn't want wooden floors and minimalist modern furniture.

Number four was easy to find, with its net

curtains and drab brown paint. There was no bell but there was a brass knocker and I had to knock several times before an aggressive 'Who is it?' answered.

'It's Kate. Inspector Todman asked me to call.'

I could hear a bolt being drawn back and then the door opened a fraction, to reveal a tiny wispy-haired old lady with two black eyes and a huge lip. 'Well, don't stand there looking gormless, girl – come on in.'

I followed through to the back room, where a coal fire burned and a large flat-screen TV blared out adverts. The shabby furniture was too big for the room, and the flower design on the wallpaper had faded long ago. Under the TV I noticed she had a DVD player and a video. 'Bloody noise,' she said. 'They always make the adverts loud – that's so they still catch us if we dare to get up to make a cup of tea.' She switched the volume down but not off. 'It's company,' she said. 'Now, sit yerself down, girl, and I'll make us a cup of tea.'

'I'll do it,' I said. She looked so frail that a draught from the front door could knock her over, and her eyes were so swollen she could hardly see. 'You sit down,' she said firmly. 'I like to keep busy – there's not many I make a brew for these days.'

So I sat down and a few minutes later she

reappeared almost staggering under the weight of a tray laden with a teapot, cups and saucers, fruitcake and biscuits.

'You pour the tea,' she said. 'And I'll cut us a nice piece of cake. You can't beat a nice bit of fruitcake, can you?'

I nodded and smiled, although when I saw the size of the slice, even I quailed. Betty's portion was equally large and she had to eat slowly because of her swollen mouth, but there was a grim determination about the way that she was dealing with the cake. I realized then she was tough, tenacious and formidable. 'I love my food,' she said. 'I never put an ounce on. I don't know where it goes. It doesn't settle, that's for sure.'

When I finished the cake, she tried to persuade me to have biscuits as well, but I refused quite firmly. 'You know your own mind,' she said. 'Do you live alone?'

I explained about Hubert and my agency. 'Well, well, I've never met a private dick before. I bet you're a tough cookie.'

I laughed. 'Nowhere near as tough as you.'

'I've 'ad to be. I've 'ad it tough most of my life. It's got easier now. It's just the loneliness that gets me down.'

'What about the ... attack?' I asked. I didn't want to say the word 'rape'.

She wiped a crumb from her mouth and then stood up and poked the fire. Not turning, she said, 'These things 'appen. It's not the first time, but at my age I didn't expect it to 'appen again.'

'Do you want to talk about it?'

''Course I do. I'll talk all night. I don't get out much these days. My legs aren't what they were. When I was younger, I could walk miles, but not any more.'

'Have you got any relatives?'

'Not as such, thank God. My family was the lowest of the low. But I've got a nephew. He's OK. I wouldn't trust him not to nick me purse, but he's got a kind heart.'

'Do you see him very often?'

'Once a week he comes round, sometimes twice. He works as a bingo caller in Birmingham. I keep late hours and sometimes he comes to see me when he's finished. He stays the night then, because he knows he'll get a good breakfast in the morning.'

'Does he have a key?'

She shook her head. 'No one has my key. If the worst 'appens to me, it 'appens. Best die quick than linger on.'

'What happened on the night you were attacked?'

She put her head on one side as if listening. 'I 'eard the doorknocker. Startled me a bit. It was about one in the morning and I was ready for bed as soon as the late-night film finished. I was a bit suspicious, because it wasn't our Terry's usual rat-a-tat-tat. But when I got to the door, he said, "It's only me, Auntie Betty." So I opened the door.'

'You were that sure it was his voice?'

'It sounded like him – my hearing's good. I was dumbstruck when this bloke all dressed in black, with one of them balaclavas covering his face, barged in and started dragging me into the bedroom. I kicked his shins but I'd only got me slippers on, so I don't reckon he felt it.'

'Did he say anything?'

'He did. He said, "It's no good struggling, Auntie Betty. Be a good girl and I won't hurt you".'

'What did you do?'

'I punched 'im in the goolies and tried to twist them off.'

'And that was when he hit you?'

Betty nodded and stared out from beneath her swollen lids. 'I wasn't surprised. I 'urt 'im. I knew then I couldn't put up a real fight, so I went as limp as month-old celery and tried to write me shopping list in me 'ead.'

I smiled. Betty was amazing.

'I've told the police what I noticed about 'im – not fat – quite well muscled. My sight's poor but I'm sure he 'ad 'airy legs. I made a grab at 'im and he was wearing one of them fleecy black tracksuits. Another thing – and I notice these things – he smelt clean. Like he'd had a shower. And I reckon he'd used one of them smelly softeners in his washing.'

'Did he say anything?'

'When he'd finished, he said, "don't tell anyone, Auntie Betty, or I'll be back."'

'He didn't say he'd kill you?'

'No.'

'What did you do then?'

'I heard the front door click and then I got up and bolted it. Then I ran myself a hot bath – it was a bit too hot and I felt near to passing out. And then I looked at myself in the mirror. What a mess! Two days later I reported it to the police.'

'Why didn't you ring the police straight away, Betty?'

She gave me a stern look. 'I watch TV,' she said. 'They use rape victims like you're a specimen on a slab – taking a bit here and a bit there – scrapings from under your nails. They even take your knickers. I wanted to report it, but only when I felt as fresh as a daisy.'

I couldn't argue with that. I would have probably felt the same. I wondered how common it was that victims raped in their own homes were far less likely to report it than those found outside, wandering, shocked and half naked. Anyway, all the forensics would be lost, but Betty was a good witness and might be willing to testify in court – if it was deemed that her evidence would help.

There was still one question I had to ask. 'This man sounded like your nephew,' I said cautiously. 'I know it's unlikely, but it couldn't have been him, could it?'

For a few moments she just peered at me, then she burst out laughing. 'He might be a tea leaf but he's sixteen stone and six foot four and he's not the incestuous sort.'

'I'm sorry, Betty,' I said, straight-faced. 'I didn't mean to shock you.'

'Don't you worry, love. Nothing shocks me. I used to be on the game. From the age of fourteen. Had to. I was being starved at home. I always had black eyes then. My mother treated me like a dog. No, worse than a dog. I don't reckon I was me Dad's – that's why she hated me. Anyway, one night she beat me black and blue and I thought, bugger this, I'm off. I packed a little suitcase and crept out in the middle of the night.'

'What happened?'

'I slept rough for a couple of nights and then, on the third night, I wandered into the red-light district – this was Birmingham – it was big business even in them days. Anyway, some bloke came up and asked me how much. I didn't cotton on for a few minutes. I'd hardly 'ad a wash in two days. Anyway, he said he'd give me two quid. That was a lot of money in those days. Like a week's wages for some people. So he took me up an alleyway and did it. He was quite nice. I think he felt sorry for me. He gave me an extra half-crown. It hurt a little bit and I bled, but I could eat and get a bath in the public baths. Next night, I was there again, and this time I met the bloke who became my pimp. I didn't know that's what he was at first, mind. I soon found out. He found me a room. It was a brothel, of course, but I kept it clean and I had plenty to eat. He taught me the tricks of the trade. Putting a bit of sponge inside me, so as I didn't get pregnant. He taught me about the kinks some men have – I could keep going all night on that one. I was on the game for ten years, but I was crafty, I managed to save a bit. My bloke got stabbed to death one night and I knew that next in line was a right thug, so I got out.' She sighed deeply, as if tiring, and shifted her position in the chair.

'Do you want to go to bed?' I asked.

'No, I don't,' she said, glancing at the clock. 'Far too early. I'll be going for the long sleep soon enough.'

For a while, she closed her eyes and seemed to forget I was there. Then, squinting at me, she said cheerfully, 'Fancy a drop of port?'

I nodded. She insisted on getting the bottle

and glasses from a small cabinet, and once we'd settled down with our half tumbler of port, she began to reminisce again. 'I left Brum and came to Longborough. I found work where I could live in – pubs, farms, and posh houses. Even did a bit of gardening. One place I worked at, I was like an au pair. The missus was a miserable old sow, but her 'usband, he was a good-looking man. A real charmer. I fell for him, of course, but in the end I had to go. What was the name of that place ... my memory 'as started to slip.' Then she laughed. 'Bit like the rest of me.'

She sipped at her port. 'Funny, innit?' she said thoughtfully. 'You'd think I'd 'ate men, being on the game and everything, but it's women I don't trust. My mum was an 'orrible bitch. Me dad 'ad his moments, but not like 'er.'

Betty closed her eyes and drifted off to sleep. I sipped at my port and then felt my eyelids begin to droop.

'Fancy falling asleep!' she said loudly. I roused myself. 'I've been thinking,' she said. 'This rapist bloke. 'E's a pervert, that's for sure. 'Is kink is old ladies. It's the opposite of those blokes who go after kiddies. Twisted, they are. But if you want to catch 'im, I'll tell you 'ow to do it.'

Nine

I waited. I really hoped Betty was going to come up with a good idea, because I sorely needed one.

'I reckon,' she said slowly. 'This man is a local pervert. He could pick on oldies because they'd be too scared to report being raped.'

'How will that help catch him?'

She peered at me. 'There's one thing I noticed about 'im, and that's 'cos I've had the experiences I've 'ad. I didn't tell you before, but I'm telling you now – he's a man with a very small dick – and I mean small.'

I sat open-mouthed for a moment. 'Yes, but the police can't examine every suspect.'

'Why not?' she asked. 'They do worse to them what's carrying drugs.'

'Yes,' I agreed. 'But what if they had two suspects who were less than well endowed.'

'Get you!' laughed Betty. 'You too posh to call a dick a dick? I'm telling you, a dick that size, you'd 'ave to see at least a hundred before you saw one as small.'

'Even erect?' I croaked.

She nodded.

I looked on Betty with renewed respect. She was wily and streetwise. Who needed a profiler? She knew about men in highly charged sexual situations. She knew their 'kinks' – their weaknesses – and she kept abreast of the times. 'I'd like your opinion,' I said. 'I think you might be able to help me.'

She smiled and looked pleased. 'Fire away, girl.'

'Do you think the man who raped you could also be the murderer of Zoe and Alice?'

Betty stared at her bony hands and then slowly shook her head. 'Nah. I reckon the rapist isn't that violent.'

'You think that, even though he gave you black eyes and a huge lip?' I asked, trying to keep my surprise low-key.

'Yeah. He punched me in retaliation. I think he was scared of me. He could have finished me off if he'd wanted to. Do you want to know what I think about 'im?'

'Of course. You're being very helpful.'

'He's a geezer who fancies old ladies. Not so many of them about – not like kiddy-fanciers. That's the only way he can manage to have sex with them. An old lady with poor sight and scared half to death isn't going to take any notice of the size of his dick.'

'What about Alice, though? She was only in her fifties.'

'Dunno,' said Betty. 'Unless it was personal. Know what I mean?'

I did know what she meant, and from then until the early hours, I listened to Betty's life story related so vividly that I forgot all about rapists and murderers, and it was only when my eyes began to close that Betty suggested I should go to bed.

The bedroom was small, with faded cornflowers on faded wallpaper. The bed itself had a wooden headboard and the bedclothes were circa 1950s, with cotton sheets, blankets and an eiderdown. The room was cold and, after a perfunctory wash in a cold bathroom, I climbed into bed still half dressed. The lumpy feather pillow with its stark white pillow case felt only slightly less cold than the bed itself. Gradually I warmed up, and my last dream of the night, of walking dark streets pursued by a man in black, was broken by the smell of bacon cooking.

I dressed quickly, brushed my hair and went downstairs. 'You're a late starter,' said Betty. 'It's past nine.' Her wispy hair stuck up at odd angles, but I noticed her eyes were more open and her lip far less swollen. She wore an apron and was busy with a frying pan. 'Don't stand about,' she said. 'Sit down, it's ready now.'

I sat down at the kitchen table and she thrust a full plate under my nose. It was the biggest breakfast I'd ever seen. 'Known for my breakfasts, I am,' she said as she sat down with an equally large plateful. 'Best meal of the day,' she muttered as she picked up a large slice of fried bread in her fingers. If I were wise, this would be the only meal of my day.

When we'd finally finished eating and she was pouring yet more tea, she said, 'What are you doing next on the case?'

I sighed, partly because I was full to busting and partly because I didn't have an answer.

'I'm only an amateur,' I said. 'This case is too big for me. I don't think I should get involved.'

'Bit late for that, love,' she said.

'I've been looking for some sort of connection between the victims.'

'Rape or murder?' Betty asked sharply.

'The rape victims. He could be the killer.'

'He's not yer killer. If you ask me, you should be looking at what the old ladies were doing years ago. The answer always lies in the past.'

'You think he planned the rapes?'

'Could be.'

'What's your connection then, Betty?'

She looked puzzled. 'I've been awake half

the night,' she said. 'But I haven't thought of anything. My memory is not as good as it was. But I will remember. You keep in touch with me, love. It's just a matter of time. Something's niggling at me – know what I mean?'

I gave her both my phone numbers and left soon after ten thirty, promising to keep in touch. I'd already checked her back door and told her not to answer the door to anyone, even if they did sound like her nephew. She'd laughed and waved me off. She was one tough old bird and she'd given me more than food. She'd given me new motivation.

I drove over to Farley Wood hoping to talk to Alvira, but there was no one in. I did have a key, but it didn't seem right to use it, so I sat in my car for an hour growing bored, and decided to try carer Annie instead. I drove back to Longborough but Annie too was out. My motivation began to dribble away.

Back at Humberstone's, Hubert was about to have lunch before his next funeral. He offered to make me a sandwich and looked slightly worried when I refused. 'Are you ailing?' he asked, as he always did if I refused any form of sustenance. I explained about the breakfast. 'If there's a source of food, you'll find it,' he said. 'Pity you can't root out a good lead.'

'Maybe I have.'

'The old girl was helpful then?'

'She was great. Better than a profiler. After all, she was there.'

'So she recognized him?'

'Not exactly.'

'What does that mean?' asked Hubert, getting a little irritated.

'She noticed something about him.'

'What?'

'Well...' I hesitated. I just knew Hubert would blush or get flustered. But I had to tell him anyway. 'In Betty's words – he's got a small dick. Small as in extremely small.'

'How would she know?'

'She's very experienced.'

'You mean, she was a bit of a goer?'

I stood staring at him, my mind whirring. 'Do you know, Hubert, sometimes you say the profoundest things.'

'Don't get sarky,' he snapped.

'No, I'm not taking the piss. That comment means something. Betty says the answer lies in the past. Ivy, Alvira, Alice and Betty were all young once. Maybe they all had a chequered past.'

'Even religious Ivy?'

'Perhaps she got religion late in life.'

Hubert didn't look convinced. 'So where do you go from here?'

'It's back to Alice's past. She's the youngest. At least her contemporaries will still be alive. Harry and co. will have some background. And you must have got records of her past employment.'

A look of vague discomfort crossed Hubert's face. 'She worked in the Co-op's funeral department for three years. Before that she had a variety of jobs.'

'What sort of jobs?'

'I didn't ask. She was a single woman with undertaking experience, and I liked her. Some people you have to take on trust.'

I couldn't argue with that. He'd taken me on as a lodger, and although I had given him the name of two referees, he hadn't taken them up.

As Hubert put on his black funeral jacket, he said, 'What you said about their pasts – this rapist, maybe murderer, couldn't be a pensioner, could he?'

That thought had crossed my mind. 'He could,' I said slowly. 'But neither Betty nor Alvira thought he was old. Betty noticed he was hairy.'

'Should be a piece of cake then, in a naked line-up,' said Hubert, giving sleepy Jasper a pat on the head.

Once Hubert had gone, I said in that loud jolly voice saved for dogs, 'Come on, Jasper – walkies!' Jasper sprang into demented

106

snapping at the lead that hung from the kitchen door, and together we braved the great outdoors. Jasper pulled excitedly and wanted to walk fast at least until we hit a tree or a patch of grass, then it was time for some serious sniffing. I shivered as I stood waiting for Jasper to distinguish smells. The clouds were low, with a variegated drabness that reminded me of the inside of a down-and-out's coat.

Eventually we reached the Co-op funeral parlour. There were white blinds at the window and glimpses of urns and flowers. The receptionist sat in a small office just off the reception area. The door was open and I walked in. Her name badge read Daphne. Grey-haired and with a comfortable shelf of a bosom, she was knitting something small in blue. 'For my grandson,' she said as she slipped it into the desk drawer. It was then that she caught sight of Jasper, who'd been behaving impeccably. There followed some fussing, and Jasper, who rarely discriminates between humans, played to his audience with much tail-wagging and hand-licking. Daphne was obviously special, because he wanted to sit on her lap, and she was more than ready to oblige. 'You're Kate from Humberstone's, aren't you? Is it about poor Alice?'

'Did you know her?'

'Yes, dear. We were quite good friends.'

'I guessed you would be,' I said. 'Alice was a very friendly person.'

'Yes, but she was a bit reserved.'

'How do you mean?'

'Alice worked here for two and a half years and never talked about her past. She talked about Harry though.'

'Harry wanted to marry her, didn't he?' I asked.

Daphne watched me steadily. 'Yes. She said he did, but she wasn't keen on marriage.'

'Is that why she remained single?'

'I don't know,' she said sharply. So sharply that she obviously did.

'Had you met Harry?'

'Once or twice.'

'Did you like him?'

Daphne shrugged. 'He seemed a nice bloke.'

'You don't sound too sure,' I said.

'I think Harry may have been her problem.'

'Problem?' I echoed.

'I don't like to say this, but I think she was scared of him,' said Daphne. 'He liked a drink, did Harry.'

'Did you ever meet him?'

'Not socially, if you know what I mean. But I used to buy sandwiches from Harry's

108

Place, and sometimes, if it wasn't busy, we'd have a coffee together.'

'What did you talk about?'

'Funny you should ask that...' She broke off. 'Do you fancy a cup of tea?'

I didn't, but I wanted to keep her talking, so I said yes. A table in the corner was already laid with cups and saucers and two of those large Thermos flasks with spouts. As she handed me the tea and a plate of biscuits, she said, 'We always have tea and biscuits available for the clients. Mind you, I eat most of them. I was an eight-stone weakling when I started work here.' She broke up a biscuit for Jasper, who sat to attention and took his share.

'When was that?'

'Thirty-five years ago.'

I kept my amazement that anyone should work in the same place for that long to myself.

'So, you must know quite a few people?' I asked.

She smiled, 'Yes. Dead and alive.'

'What about Ivy Trees?'

'I know the name,' she said. 'Something's stirring in the grey matter. A bit of a scandal – well, for these parts anyway.'

'What sort of scandal?'

Daphne looked at me quizzically. 'What's this got to do with Alice? I thought that's why you were here.'

'It is. But there have been some ... nasty happenings ... in Longborough, and I've been looking for connections.'

'Aren't the police doing that?'

'Yes, but Hubert was very fond of Alice, and if I can find out who murdered her—'

'I can understand that,' she interrupted, 'but what has Ivy Trees got to do with all this?'

I shrugged. 'I've got no idea yet.'

Daphne began eating another biscuit. I felt I'd alienated her. She must have known Ivy was dead, and perhaps she thought I was merely gossip-mongering. After a few moments, I said, 'What did you mean about Alice being scared of Harry?'

'I shouldn't have said that,' she snapped. 'I don't think Harry killed her, so don't get the wrong idea.'

'Have you any ideas who might have killed her?'

An expression of mild incredulity crossed her face. 'Of course I haven't.' She paused for a moment. 'Alice was a friend of mine and I don't want her name dragged through the mire.'

'Why should it be?'

'I'm sorry,' she said. 'I told the police everything I know about Alice. She wasn't very forthcoming, and if she did keep some things to herself – well, why not?'

I knew it was time to go when she took out her knitting from the drawer. I thanked her and left.

On the way back to Humberstone's, I talked it through with Jasper. He wagged his tail at appropriate moments, so it felt worthwhile. Alice still seemed the odd one out amongst the victims. Zoe had been killed near her home. If the killer/rapist were the same person and had already gained access to Alice's house, why had he risked killing her in the town? What was Daphne trying to hide? Obviously there was someone in Alice's past who might shed light on her murderer, but it seemed all roads led to Harry.

Later that evening, I tried ringing David, but he wasn't answering his mobile, so I left a message for him to ring me. He rang me about an hour later. I told him about my visit to Betty and he said, 'We're working on it, Kate. Don't forget, we can't breach anyone's human rights – examining private parts probably constitutes that.'

'Yes. But you do believe her?'

'We do.'

'Are you looking for one man or two?'

'Our profiler thinks two men are involved.'

'What about Alice?' I asked.

'What about her?'

'She doesn't fit. Neither young nor old. Killed by battering in a fairly public place.'

'I didn't tell you this before,' he said. 'But we do know from the post-mortem that Alice had a baby. The pathologist can't tell when, but many years ago. We don't know yet if the child is still alive, but we're finding out. As soon as I know anything, I'll let you know.'

I was about to put the phone down when he added, 'By the way, Harry's gone missing.'

Ten

When Hubert came in later, Jasper did his circles of delight routine, where he chases his tail and then licks Hubert's shoes. I bombarded Hubert with information and he looked from one to the other of us, fussed Jasper for a few seconds and then announced he was having a bath and would it be too much trouble for me to put the kettle on. He didn't seem a bit surprised about Harry, so he obviously knew more than I did, but wasn't prepared to share that knowledge with me, so I didn't ask.

Hubert appeared in the kitchen half an hour later, wearing a black tracksuit. 'Going jogging?' I asked.

'We'll be going out later,' he said as he picked up his mug of tea that I'd just poured. As Hubert was not exactly a man of mystery, I waited for more info. 'I've contacted a glazier.'

'Are we having new windows put in? It's about time. But why do we have to go out?'

'We're not having new windows put in. A

small window is being taken out.'

'Where? Why?' I glanced swiftly at Hubert's face. He looked shifty. 'What are you up to?'

'Nothing,' he said. 'How about you cooking tonight?'

'Me! Do you think I can manage?'

'Just get on with it and I might tell you why I'm doing your job.'

If it's possible to be intrigued and irritated at the same time – I was both. I clattered about, preparing prawns and bacon with chilli. I managed to squash down spaghetti into a large pan of boiling water without scalding my wrists, and opened a bottle of wine. 'You're driving, I suppose,' I said. At this point I was on the verge of giving Hubert the silent treatment.

We sat down to eat. After two mouthfuls, Hubert said, 'This meal is ruddy awful. What did you put the chilli in with – a trowel?' He was right about the meal being awful, and while he threw his in the bin and made cheese on toast, I manfully ate the hot-as-hell meal I'd cooked. I longed to ask what his comment about doing my job was all about, but I wasn't going to give him the satisfaction.

He washed up and I dried in total silence. This sort of atmosphere isn't so unusual among those living together in a proper relationship. It troubled me. More and more, we were becoming like an old married couple who, all passion spent, find little ways of irritating each other to try to reignite a spark. Hubert and I had never had a spark, and I was beginning to realize, as my thirties were fast speeding past, that it was time for me to make a whole new life. We were far too comfortable. He was too much of a shoulder to lean on. In fact, we were holding each other back. As I drank another glass of wine, I resolved that, once this case was sorted, I would make plans to leave Longborough.

The drive to my unknown destination was short. In fact, it was just to the edge of the oldest part of Longborough. A few streets of terraced houses with small back gardens and a grass-verged alleyway between them. I'd wandered this way once before with Jasper, who was a keen grass-verge sniffer.

Hubert parked his car under a street lamp and murmured, 'It's number three.'

Still I remained silent. As we walked to the top of the deserted road, I noticed the street sign – Regal Street. The houses were well cared for, but it certainly wasn't 'regal'. By now, the penny having taken some time to drop, I realized number three had been Alice's home. I broke the silence and spoke in a whisper, 'What about the police?'

'Wasn't the scene of the crime, so the search didn't take long,' he replied.

'It was the scene of a rape.'

'Ah – but the forensics team have already done their fingerprinting and samples.'

'You're in the know,' I said. I was peeved because it seemed to me that Hubert was getting inside information. 'Have you been speaking to David?' I asked.

'Might have,' he said. Hubert wasn't a good liar, so 'might have' meant an unequivocal yes. I didn't have any claims on David, but I objected to Hubert taking over my role.

Number three had a paved front garden with pots of false greenery. The windows and front door were white, and all the curtains were drawn. I followed Hubert to the alleyway around the back of the house. Hubert produced a torch from his jacket pocket, because the houses on either side were in darkness and the night sky was cloudy and moonless. The back gate creaked slightly and a dog began to bark. 'Do you think this is a good idea?' My voice was a mere whisper. Guilt, I supposed, had that effect. Usually Hubert was the voice of caution, but it was me that now had a real sense of foreboding. Someone could be watching us. Some 'have a go' hero might just want to take us on.

We crept up the garden path to the accompaniment of the barking dog. It wasn't a long garden and there were no obstacles in our way. At the back door, Hubert stopped. All the windows were closed. Now what? Hubert turned to me with a sly grin, put his hand on the door handle and said, 'Open Sesame.' And it did.

'How did you do that?' I asked. 'Where did you get a key from?'

'No key,' he said. 'My willing glazier. He just took a glass panel out of the door, put his hand through and the keys were on the inside. He opened the door, replaced the pane and left us access.'

'A bit careless of the police to leave the keys in the door,' I commented. 'Unless, of course, it was deliberate.'

'Stop whingeing and come inside,' said Hubert, giving me a little shove.

Once inside, Hubert pulled down the kitchen blind and switched on the light. Convenient, I thought, that the power was still on, but I guessed that it was either an oversight like the keys in the back door, or the police had no powers to switch off services without the permission of the owner or next of kin and beneficiary. It didn't really matter, but I still didn't know what Hubert hoped to achieve by this unlawful entry.

I looked around the kitchen. There was a breakfast bar, empty save for a bowl of fast-decaying fruit. The floor tiles were a pale lime green which matched the units. On the windowsill were pots of herbs. Herbs that were still vigorous. I touched the earth in the herb pots – it was still moist. 'Someone's watered these today,' I said.

'It doesn't surprise me,' said Hubert, nodding to the door that led away from the kitchen.

We peered into the two living rooms without putting on the lights. Everything was clean and tidy. Eerily so. There seemed to be no sign of Alice's personality, almost as if she'd been planning to move, depersonalizing her home as the TV pundits suggested. Was she in fact planning to sell up and leave Harry? Had he lost his temper when he found out?

Having wandered around the house, I noticed Hubert wasn't delving into any drawers or cupboards. 'What exactly are we doing here?' I asked.

'You'll see,' he said. 'Come on, let's go down to the cellar.'

In the hall, the door I'd assumed was a cupboard was in fact the door to the cellar. The key was still in the lock. Hubert opened the door, flicked the light switch and yelled, 'Come up, Harry, we know you're down there! You'll be OK.'

There was no response. 'Harry!' he yelled again. 'It's only Kate and me. Nothing to worry about.'

118

From below came a sort of scrabbling noise. I immediately thought rats. Hubert began the descent and reluctantly I followed him. We'd gone several steps down when suddenly a man wearing a black hooded jacket barged past us. It was so unexpected, even more so as he kicked me hard in the back of the knee and I fell on to Hubert and we went hurtling down the stairs.

I'd had a soft landing but Hubert was groaning. I groaned inwardly. Cellars, in my experience, had always been bad news. I eased myself off Hubert and asked if he was hurt. 'Crushed. I've been bloody crushed,' he muttered as he tried to sit upright. 'You weigh a ton.' I helped him sit up, which he managed without crying out, so I presumed nothing much was broken. 'Forget the insults,' I said. 'Are you OK?'

'I would be if I wasn't on a cellar floor – locked in.'

'No problem,' I said. 'I've got my mobile. I'll ring David.'

I rang him. There was a problem. He was in a meeting and he'd be another half-hour or so.

'Half an hour,' I said. 'What's half an hour spent with a good friend in a damp cellar?'

'Too long,' said Hubert. 'Can't you smell it?' He was looking up towards the gap under the cellar door. Now I could both smell it and see it. Smoke was beginning to creep in, and now I was sure I could hear the crackle of flames. My hands trembled as I pressed nine-nine-nine. My voice sounded as if I was already choking on the smoke, but the operator's voice calmed me a little. 'Stay low,' she said. 'The fire brigade is on its way. Do you want to stay on the line?' I didn't. The very last thing I wanted was to die on the line.

We crawled over to a corner of the cellar. Then we lay down looking towards the stairs. The smoke was ever increasing. Hubert began murmuring the Lord's Prayer, as he always did in times of crisis. 'Hedging my bets,' he muttered. Then he added, 'Be brave,' and patted my shoulder. Tears welled in my eyes. I glanced at my watch. Three minutes had gone by since my call to the fire brigade. Another three and the door might begin to burn through, and then the smoke really would come pouring in. If I had just a few minutes left, who would I ring on my mobile? Sadly I realized there was no one I could inflict that on. No one special person would need, really need, to know that I loved him or her. And now there was no time to change that.

'Who the hell was that bastard in the cellar?' I asked. Anger, I reasoned, was better than sad and maudlin.

'It wasn't Harry, that's for sure.'

Hubert handed me a clean linen handkerchief. 'It might come in handy,' he said. I clenched the hankie in my hand and watched as the filthy grey smoke increased in volume. I rested my head on Hubert's shoulder. There was nothing we could do.

Eleven

I'd sunk into an apathetic acceptance of our fate during the next minute or so, when my mobile phone, still clutched in my hand, rang.

'Is that Kate?'

I didn't recognize the voice at first, but I agreed that I was Kate – but only just.

'You sound strange,' she said. 'It's Jade from the Crown.'

'I'm in a difficult position...' I began croakily.

'Yeah, well, so am I. I need to see you. Can you come in today?'

I didn't or couldn't answer.

'Well, can you? Leave it too long and I might change my mind.'

'Jade,' I began with amazing calmness. 'I'm trapped in the cellar of a burning house, smoke is pouring in and the fire brigade is meant to be on its way.'

'Straight up? You're not winding me up?'

'No. I'm telling the truth.'

'Gawd! Anything I can do?'

'I wish there was.'

'Where are you? What's the address?' Jade was shouting so loudly that I had to hold my mobile away from my ear. I told her the address. 'Is there a window or a grille or something?' she yelled. Then, more quietly, adding, 'Don't you give up.'

'I don't know...'I began, meaning that we hadn't looked for a window or a grille, but the line was already dead.

Hubert had caught the whole conversation, and he began looking for a window or a grille. Neither of us had taken in our surroundings. One cellar seeming much the same as another. This one had whitewashed stone walls speckled with green mould. In one corner were several large cardboard boxes, sealed and covered in polythene. Together we dragged the boxes from the wall. There, sure enough, was a rusty grille. The size of which would accommodate my two feet side by side. But there was some fresh air. However, would the extra oxygen feed or even encourage the fire?

I checked my watch again. Fear had altered time. Minutes seemed like hours. My ears were on full alert for the sound of sirens. I thought of Jasper. If the worst happened, would he settle in another home or an animal sanctuary? Then I remembered that Megan liked dogs. I was fairly sure that she would take care of him, and that was a comfort.

The smoke was making me cough now. I grabbed Hubert's hand. He squeezed mine back. His face was a yellow grey.

Suddenly I heard voices from outside. 'Oi, love – get back from that grille. We're going to get you out.' I wriggled back and caught a glimpse of mud-stained boots. Whoever he was, he wasn't a fireman. Then began the sounds of pickaxes being swung. We moved further back as dust and debris swirled around.

It seemed, as hope surged in us, that only a couple of minutes passed before a big hole had formed. The grille had gone and beefy arms were dragging me out into the fresh air. Hubert followed, swift as afterbirth, and we were led away from the rubble by our three saviours.

As we got to the front of the house, half of Longborough seemed to be watching the fire in their pyjamas and dressing gowns. I soon heard the rumours that circulated as swift as the smoke. There was another fire in town. Harry's house was burning, and it had spread to the house next door, where children were trapped. I think I was in shock, but I managed to thank our rescuers, two of whom were already on their way to offer their assistance. The remaining one, short, bald and stocky, wearing only a tight tee shirt and jeans, said, 'I'm Jade's uncle. You'd better thank her. She interrupted our after-hours game of darts.' Hubert and I thanked him profusely and I offered up even more thanks to Jade for her presence of mind.

Three fire appliances arrived then, and I rushed over to a likely looking senior officer to say we were out and safe and well.

Then the police arrived, David being among them. 'What about the other fire?' I asked before he had time to say anything. 'Are the children out?' He nodded. 'Some smoke inhalation. They've gone to hospital.'

All the emergency services seemed to have arrived at once, and David led us to an ambulance, insisting that we needed to be checked out. Hubert's colour had improved only a little and he was given oxygen straight away, which soon brought back his normal sallow complexion.

David wanted to take us straight home, but I wanted to see Jade, not only to thank her, but to find out what she had to tell me. 'She's got information,' I said.

'All right. My arm is twisted. I'll get it cleared with Waterworth.'

He rang 'Twice' on his mobile phone and I could hear Waterworth's response loud and clear. Even his four-letter expletives were delivered twice.

'No problem,' said David calmly, as he switched off his boss's hectoring voice. 'Bastard!' he added as he took my arm and led me and Hubert to his car.

At the Crown pub, the door was locked, but we could hear voices from inside. It was Jade who answered the door. I thanked her and gave her a hug.

'Glad you're all right,' she said. 'My uncle says it was a near thing.'

'Your uncle and his mates are heroes.'

'They've just come in. You can buy them a drink.'

Hubert, feeling more than grateful to be alive, said magnanimously, 'All the drinks are on us.' I grinned when we walked into the pub lounge. It was packed. News that the Crown was open after hours had obviously spread, and now there was standing room only. Jade whispered to me that she'd see me later, but in private. David, it seemed, was not to be included in the information.

As David waited at the bar, Hubert said, 'David's really keen on you. He looked worried sick at the house.'

'You're imagining things,' I said. I felt flattered though. He had seemed attentive, and he was here with us, when Waterworth had ordered him to 'get your arse here – not later, now ... now!' David Todman was definitely going up in my estimation. Even more so when he returned with a double brandy for us and drank Coke himself.

I'd just finished my drink and my hands and knees had stopped trembling. It was David who had noticed; I was too euphoric at being out of that damn cellar. He put an arm around me and said, 'You're looking better now, Kate. Except for your dirty face.' I was mortified and rushed off to the Ladies. Sure enough, I had black streaks on my cheeks, a mixture of mascara and smoke dust. I was just drying my face under the hot-air dryer when Jade came in.

'I can't stop long,' she said. 'We're so busy, but I had to tell you something about Zoe.'

'What about her?'

'Zoe had a boyfriend. An older guy. He used to meet her in secret. I'm not sure ... but that story about being followed and attacked may have been a pack of lies. She had it in readiness in case she was late home.'

'Why didn't you tell me this before? She's dead. Why lie?'

Jade shrugged. 'I suppose I'll have to tell you. This guy – I fancy him – or I did. He comes in the pub and I'd fancied him for ages. He seemed to like me, sort of chatted me up, but then I found out he was seeing Zoe. When she was murdered, I thought...'

'You thought you could step into her

shoes?'

'Yeah ... but then I thought maybe he was the one who killed her. I don't want to get done for withholding evidence.'

Jade looked genuinely worried.

'I won't tell anyone,' I said. 'But you must give me his name and address.'

Her reluctance only lasted seconds. 'I don't know where he lives, but his name is Stewart Walker.' Then she added, almost in a whisper, 'He could be married.'

Back in the lounge bar, both Hubert and David looked at me strangely. 'What's going on?' asked David.

'Nothing,' I said. 'Just washing my face.'

'Well, I've got some news,' he said. 'I've just heard from Waterworth. It's a major breakthrough. The bloke who set fire to Alice's house is her son. He's our prime suspect for Alice's murder, and probably the rapes.'

'Has he confessed?'

'Not yet, but it seems he has a long psychiatric history – paranoid schizophrenia.'

'That doesn't make him a rapist and a murderer,' I said. 'He could just be an arsonist. Has he confessed to arson?'

David flashed me an irritated look. 'I don't know yet. I should be in the interview room finding out.'

'Don't let me stop you.'

Hubert intervened then. 'Don't spoil the end of a wonderful day, Kate. We've had a miraculous escape, and with any luck, Alice's murderer has been found and Harry's in the clear. In my opinion, a very good result...'

I didn't agree, but I shut up then. I didn't mention Jade's info to David. That would have to wait, and maybe I could save him some trouble.

My euphoria hadn't lasted; perhaps the brandy had dampened it down. Now all I wanted was a warm bed and my duvet. A few minutes later, it was Hubert who suggested we go. As I stood up, I felt dizzy and David had to take my arm and negotiate me through the door.

Back at Humberstone's, he insisted on taking me to my room. He left me sitting on the bed but kissed me goodnight. I'd quite hoped he would undress me but I probably wasn't thinking straight. I took off my jeans and shoes and slipped under the duvet. The room seemed to spin for a while and unbidden came memories of being in the cellar.

When I woke, I panicked for a few seconds until I realized that the hot, stuffy, airless atmosphere was due only to the fact that the duvet was over my head. It was morning, the light was flooding into the room and I felt glad to be alive.

Twelve

My feel-good factor didn't last. As the day went on, I developed a headache, had occasional shivering episodes and – worse – flashbacks. Around eleven a.m. I decided I needed to be lying down. I couldn't concentrate on even the most trivial of morning TV, so I crept back into bed and within seconds I was asleep, only to relive in my dreams the horror of being trapped in that cellar.

When I woke up it was growing dark and Hubert stood by my bed holding a mug of tea and looking worried. 'It's three o'clock,' he said. 'Are you ill?'

My head still throbbed and my eyes seemed blurred and then I started to cough. 'You need a doctor,' said Hubert. 'You inhaled smoke – you look terrible.'

'I'll be OK.' I said. 'What can a doctor do for me? I'll get over it.'

Hubert didn't look pleased. 'Had you eaten anything?'

'I've had a slice of toast,' I said. I didn't tell him that I'd burnt the toast and the smell and sight of it had made me vomit.

'What do you fancy for supper?' he asked.

'I'll be fine with the tea,' I said.

It was the wrong answer. Hubert looked even more worried, but he sloped off as I started drinking his tea.

During the evening, I was most definitely in the twilight zone. I lay on the sofa drifting in and out of TV programmes that barely registered. I fell asleep again, my sleep punctuated by nightmares and the sound of the phone ringing. When I woke, greyish light had seeped into my room and, although I assumed it was morning, I felt that I'd lost a day of my life. My headache was a little less intense and, although I coughed on my way to the bathroom, it didn't rack my body. I was on the mend, I told myself as I staggered in my dressing gown towards the smell of breakfast.

Hubert stood in the kitchen watching the eye-level grill. He had a tray ready for me – tinned grapefruit and cornflakes. 'This looks good,' I said. 'I'm starving.'

'You're looking better,' he said, smiling.

Just as he sat down to eat his sausages and bacon, his mobile rang. He looked a little pained, so I said, 'They'll leave a message if it's important.' But he sighed, picked up his mobile phone from the table and left the room. OK, I thought, he's keeping secrets –

so I stole one of his sausages. I was still eating it when he reappeared.

'Scavenger!' he declared as he sat down to eat.

'Well?'

'Well what?' he asked, all innocence.

'What's going on?'

'What do you mean?'

'You know what I mean, Hubert. I heard the phone ringing last night and now this morning you're all secretive.'

'You don't miss a trick, do you? Even half-dead.'

'I'm not half-dead. I'm fit enough for a sausage.'

He sighed. 'It was David.'

'Enquiring after my health?'

'No...' began Hubert tentatively, 'it was about the fire. The fire officers have made an interim report.'

'And?'

'Charlie, Alice's son, used an accelerant. Paraffin, they think. It seems he made some attempt to put out the flames when he realized it wasn't Harry in the cellar. Alice, it appears, had been friendly with the family next door. So he assumed Harry was there and he lobbed a Molotov cocktail through their back window.'

'They were so lucky.'

'It wasn't just luck. The fire brigade was

132

there in three minutes.'

'Is the house livable?'

Hubert shook his head. 'No, but friends and neighbours have rallied round and the town has started a fund.'

'I'll give as much as possible,' I said.

'It's already done,' said Hubert, grinning.

'What about Charlie? Has he actually confessed?'

'In a way, but the police don't think he'll be fit to plead. David thinks he'll be shipped off to Broadmoor as soon as his psychiatric reports are complete.'

'All's well...' I began. Then stopped as I saw Hubert's expression.

'Not exactly,' said Hubert. There is something else.'

'What?'

'The fire investigation officer is coming to see us today.'

'What about?'

'I'm not sure. Give us a bollocking, I suppose.'

'What time?'

Hubert looked at his watch. 'Half an hour or so.'

I debated with myself if it was worth rushing off and trying to look presentable, and decided that it was better to look slightly pathetic. After all, we were victims. And we'd had a key.

Promptly, half an hour later, the fire investigation officer sat in our kitchen and refused coffee. If I hadn't known his line of work, I would have thought he was a nightclub bouncer, for he had a large square shaved head, a muscular neck and a flat nose. He wore a navy suit and blue tie. When he spoke, though, his voice betrayed him. It was high-pitched and feminine. Hubert shot me a warning glance in case I didn't take the man seriously.

'Now then,' he said, flicking open a notebook and raising a gold pen. 'My name is Joseph Gardener. I have a dual role. Fire investigations, for which I'm paid, and fire prevention, for which I'm not. Be kind enough to explain to me what exactly you two were doing in the house at the time.'

Hubert explained that he was merely looking for his missing friend.

'And you thought he'd be there?'

'Yes. Obviously. We wouldn't have been there otherwise,' said Hubert, sounding aggrieved.

'Who did the house belong to?' asked Gardener.

'My friend Harry's dead girlfriend. She was murdered recently.'

'Do the police know who was responsible?'

'The same man,' said Hubert, 'who started the fire – my employee Alice's son.'

134

'What a tangled web,' said Gardener.

He then wrote down our names, address and telephone number and flicked closed his notebook. His small grey eyes looked upwards. 'Shall we test your smoke alarm before I go?'

'Well er...' began Hubert, looking uncomfortable.

'As I thought,' said Gardener. 'The battery hasn't been changed, has it? Has it? If you knew,' he continued, 'how many people die because they are too lazy to change a battery. They should have *Died through lack of a battery* engraved on their tombstone. And another thing, a business like this should have a sprinkler system. After all, the dear departed relatives wouldn't want their loved ones burned to a crisp before the service, would they? Especially those who were due for burial.'

All this was said in his high falsetto voice and with a deadpan expression. I avoided eye contact with Hubert and began to cough to hide my nervous laughter.

Eventually he left after further admonishment about our lack of working smoke alarms. 'All rooms and hallways need one,' he said as a parting warning. 'It's a matter of life and death.'

He was right, of course, but even so, I began to laugh when Hubert wagged his finger at me and said, 'Now then, Kate, don't mock the afflicted.'

It was later that morning and I was in the kitchen debating about the calorific wisdom of either baking a cake or making a batch of scones, when Hubert appeared in the doorway. His expression was serious, very serious.

'I should have told you this before, Kate, but you were out of it yesterday and you seem much better now, so I'm telling you now. And David wanted me to tell you...'

'Tell me what?' I asked impatiently.

'Another young woman has gone missing.'

I shivered. 'When? What happened?'

'Don't jump to conclusions, Kate. She's nineteen. Her name is Lianne Brooks and she lives with two girl housemates. They often don't come home at night and they didn't realize she was actually missing until her boyfriend came looking for her. He reported it to the police.'

'When was she last seen?'

'A CCTV camera caught her in the car park by the river about nine p.m. on Friday night, walking away from the river.'

'Alone?'

'Yes.'

'What was she doing there?'

Hubert shrugged. 'I don't know. David

says her friends don't know either.'

'Are they dragging the river?'

'Not yet. But there is a general search this morning.'

'What day is it anyway?' I asked.

'Sunday, of course.'

I took no notice of Hubert's surprise, but did wonder if my inhaling smoke had damaged a few more grey cells. 'I'll help in the search,' I said. 'I take it the police need all the help they can get.'

'That's debatable,' said Hubert dourly. 'The press and extra police are everywhere. Longborough is now seen as a hotbed of mayhem and madness. Lianne's disappearance is major news. She's been on every channel.'

'And the papers?'

'It's in yesterday's local,' he said, handing me Saturday's *Longborough News*.

The whole of the front page was taken up with a photo of a pretty smiling girl in school uniform. The headline in huge letters simply said MISSING. Inside, there were interviews with her housemates, her parents and her boyfriend, Mark Underwood. By their accounts, she was a fun-loving, happy girl who was enjoying a health and beauty course at a college in Birmingham and hoped in the future to become a film make-up artist. They were all adamant that she was safety-conscious. And that if she'd accepted a lift, it would only have been from someone she knew and trusted. Mentally, I added, *Or thought she knew*.

The search started at eleven, and Hubert and I decided that Jasper needed a good long walk too, so the three of us made our way towards the start of the search. The place where Lianne was last seen, near the car park by the river. It was a chilly, grey day with low foreboding clouds. The population of Longborough seemed to be on the march with us. It occurred to me that perhaps they had nothing better to do, or was that merely cynicism? I sensed in the groupings a vigilante element amongst those young shaven-haired muscular men who looked as if they'd just left a British National Party meeting. Mothers, some with children, were also making their way towards the riverside.

The procession of people were already watchful and curious. Eyes scanned towards doorways and alleys. Even Jasper seemed aware that there was a sense of urgency in the air. He trotted on ahead of us briskly, not lingering at his favourite sniffing spots.

When we arrived at the car park, it was cordoned off and 'Twice' Waterworth was there with a megaphone, looking flustered at the numbers that had turned up. 'I don't have to tell you,' he boomed. 'I don't have to tell you – keep together! The sergeant and the PC here –' he pointed to a burly uniformed officer and a young female PC – 'they will take your names and addresses in groups of six and give you a search area. No pushing, no shoving and no mothers with children. We don't want any accidents, and you undertake this search at your own risk.' He paused. 'If you do find a body ... don't touch it. I repeat: do not touch anything that might be significant. The search will end at two forty-five exactly. A quarter to three. Good luck.'

I meanwhile looked around for David and felt disappointed that he wasn't there. It took until nearly twelve for our names and addresses to be taken. Hubert and I, together with four others, including Tone and Sal, were given the riverbank itself and the small park nearby. After that, an obliging PC said we could 'please ourselves'.

Sal wore a short mock-fur coat and a fur hat with ear flaps, making her look like a Russian grandmother. Tone wore jeans and a brown check jacket with leather patches on the elbows, and in contrast to Sal, looked perished.

'You OK, Kate?' she asked. 'You were lucky to escape.'

I nodded. 'Have you heard from Harry?'

'Not a word.'

'You look as cold as I feel,' said Tone, walking alongside me and taking my arm. 'You cuddle up to me, darlin'– you'll be all right.'

It wasn't long before we'd searched one side of the river bank. In the park, a shout went up when someone found an old shoe. We gathered round to inspect it. The sole was worn through, the uppers were caked in mud and it was once a men's black lace-up, approximately a size ten. Tone laughed, 'Even my brother couldn't repair that one, and he used to be in the business.'

Having inspected every bush and behind every tree, we made our way back to the car park to report that we had found nothing. We were thanked for our efforts and decided to fan out around the town. I walked with Sal and she proved to be an expert on the lives of film stars. A great fan of soaps, she seemed to catch every episode and had an opinion on every character. I nodded and smiled but I was surprised how seriously she took fictional lives. For Sal, it seemed the dividing line between character and actor was very slim indeed. In real life, Sal lived with a cat called Peaches, she'd always worked in catering, had never wanted to marry, but she'd like to meet a man with a car who'd take her for days out.

Once it began to rain, people started drifting away from the town, and by now I guessed every alleyway, garage and wheelie bin had been checked more than once. Slight rain didn't bother either of us, but when the deluge began, we sheltered in a shop doorway and waited for it to stop. There was no sign of Hubert and Jasper, or Tone, and although it was only two thirty, the light was fast fading as the black clouds shed their load and Longborough's High Street became awash.

'Come back to my place,' suggested Sal. 'Until this lot blows over.'

Sal lived above a Chinese takeaway in one of the side streets. Although Sunday was the one day the Mayflower closed, I found the smell of cooking mixed with our dampness almost overpowering. 'It's lucky I love Chinese food,' laughed Sal.

'What about the smell?' I asked.

'I don't smell it any more,' she said.

She put our coats over a radiator, insisted on stuffing my wet shoes with newspaper, and proudly showed me round the flat. That didn't take long. There was a small open-plan kitchen and sitting room, a bedroom, where Peaches the cat sprawled unconcern-ed on the bed and framed celebrity photo-graphs stared at her from the walls. In the sitting room, soap celebrities were arranged around the room in photograph frames as if they were family members.

Sal made coffee and we sat together on a pink two-seater sofa in front of a huge TV screen, with a mock coal-effect fire warming us while Sal watched the omnibus edition of EastEnders. 'I've watched it before,' she said, 'but I do like to see it again.'

After a while of silent watching, she said, 'Tone would have liked to be a Londoner. He thinks Tone sounds more cockney than Tony.'

'He seems a nice guy,' I said.

'Yeah, he's lovely, and he's great to work with. He's always happy-go-lucky. Harry gets on with him too.'

She relapsed into silence and, to my shame, I fell asleep. When I woke up, it took me a few seconds to remember where I was. 'It's stopped raining,' she said. 'You've had a nice snooze.'

'Well, I'd better be off,' I said, standing up and looking round for my shoes and coat.

'Your Hubert will report you missing,' she said as she handed me my shoes. I had the feeling she couldn't wait for me to go, so I ignored the possessive reference to Hubert, thanked her for the coffee, apologized for falling asleep and left.

By now it was nearly six p.m. and the High Street was deserted. The street lights were reflected in the huge puddles, drains were blocked and the rain, now a desultory dribble, made the cold night even more miserable.

I hurried home, but occasionally a noise would startle me, a can moving in the gutter, the bough of a tree making a snapping sound. Then my imagination began to play tricks. I thought I heard footsteps behind me. I told myself that it was unlikely 'he' was on the loose, but I began to think about Lianne. Had she been hurrying through the town when she imagined she heard footsteps behind her? Had she kept looking back like I was doing, and yet seen no one?

It was as I walked into Humberstone's car park, and saw that Hubert was in and lights were blazing, that I relaxed. I felt in my pockets for my keys. There were none.

Then I heard a voice I recognized calling, 'Kate. Over here.' I hesitated. I swung round. I couldn't see anyone. 'Kate ... I'm over here.' The voice sounded different now. I began running towards my own front door. A scream was only a breath away.

Thirteen

I was banging frantically on the door when I felt a hand on my shoulder. Far from fighting back like a demented kick-boxer – I froze. 'You don't learn, do you, Kate?' said David, sounding angry.

I spun round. 'You bastard, you've been following me. What are you trying to do?'

'Just showing you how easy it is.'

I muttered 'bastard' again under my breath, but by now I was feeling sick but relieved. I wasn't going to show him that I was relieved, and by now Hubert was at the door saying, 'What's going on?'

'This idiot has followed me and scared me half to death. He should know better.'

'He did volunteer to find you,' said Hubert, ushering us in. 'You had no keys and no mobile.'

I stomped up the stairs muttering, 'That's no bloody excuse.'

'Don't worry,' I heard Hubert say to David. 'She'll be all right after a hot bath and some food.'

I was so mad, I did go straight to the bathroom. After a few minutes in a steaming bath, I began to calm down. Hubert came knocking on the door ten minutes later to tell me supper was being served in five minutes. David, it seemed hadn't eaten all day – as if I cared.

Hubert had opened a large tin of mushroom soup and made a pile of toasted cheese sandwiches. I have to admit my mood did improve then, and we slumped into Hubert's comfortable chairs and trawled the television stations for any news of Lianne. There wasn't any, so Hubert switched off the TV and David said, 'I know it's depressing about Lianne, but there is some news on Zoe's killing.'

'You've got a suspect?' I asked in surprise.

'We have. Her father, Graham. He's been questioned twice.'

'With a result?' I asked.

'Waterworth seems to think he's guilty, but there's no real evidence. Waterworth just doesn't like him, and he's doing his best to prove he's a religious fanatic who would stop at nothing to control his daughter.'

'What do you think?'

David thought for a moment, 'I think,' he said, 'that he's an oddball, but if we arrested every so-called oddball on mere suspicion, at least twenty per cent of the police force would be in the nick.'

'Surely Burrows isn't under suspicion for the rapes?'

David smiled. 'He'd be under suspicion for Alice's murder had we not found her son. But give it time. Waterworth doesn't like his patch being under the spotlight, and he's under a lot of pressure for a quick result.'

'What about the profiler?' asked Hubert, who placed great faith in experts.

'He's put in an appearance,' said David, not sounding too impressed. 'But he hasn't really told us anything we couldn't have worked out for ourselves. He was only called in because Waterworth jumped to the conclusion that a serial killer was at large. Now it looks as if that isn't the case...'

'Hang on,' I interrupted. 'Let's not forget poor Lianne. She could well be a victim of the rapist. Old ladies don't usually put up a fight, but if Lianne fought back or started screaming, he may have felt forced to silence her. After all, he did attack Betty. She just sensed it was best not to resist any more.'

David looked suddenly depressed and defeated. 'We're checking out all known sex offenders within a radius of fifty miles, and that takes time.'

'Are there many?'

'Don't ask, Kate. The numbers are frightening, but most are reasonably harmless.

146

Flashers, gropers, peeping toms. The rest are released rapists and paedophiles.'

'You are taking the rape of Ivy and Alvira seriously, though?'

David gazed at me with a pained expression. 'The trouble is, murder takes precedence over rape, especially unreported rape. Waterworth's priority now is finding Lianne Brooks.'

'But...' I began.

'No buts. That's the way it is,' said David. 'Alvira and Betty are witnesses, but they're both alive. We just have to carry on.'

'That means zero suspects on the rapes.'

'At the moment,' he agreed. 'But if Lianne Brooks does turn up dead, and it looks likely at the moment, then maybe the forensics team will get lucky.'

I sat for a moment staring into space. Hubert organized brandies all round, and I noticed how quiet and subdued he seemed. I would have preferred tea, but I sipped reluctantly at my brandy.

'How are the Brooks family coping?' he asked David.

'We've got a female officer staying at the parents' house,' said David. 'And the housemates have moved back to their families. They're devastated. They really can't understand what she was doing near the river, and although she was last seen walking away from the river, they fear she may have been drowned.'

David left a short time later, and as I saw him off, he hugged me rather awkwardly and unexpectedly. 'Promise me you won't walk around after dark,' he said gruffly.

'It's dark at four,' I said. 'I can't live in fear.'

'Well, you should be afraid until this is all sorted.'

When I returned to Hubert, he was still sitting in the same position looking thoughtful.

'What if she's still alive, being held somewhere?' he said miserably. 'I keep thinking of that case in France where those poor girls were held in a cellar and starved to death.'

'Please don't mention cellars,' I said. 'You'll give me nightmares.'

'Alive or dead, the police will find her,' said Hubert. 'They're drafting in extra personnel from all over the place.' Then he added despondently, 'I won't sleep tonight.' I gave him another stiff brandy and later, as I lay in bed wide awake, I wished I had joined him.

I lay awake for hours, my thoughts as tangled as a plate of overcooked spaghetti. When I did eventually sleep, I had nightmares so intense they woke me.

Daylight was pure balm and just for a few moments I forgot about the virus-like tragedies in Longborough. When I remembered, I let my thoughts drift idly towards sunnier places, and I even imagined joining my mother in the West Indies.

I sat up with a start and realized that the situation really was depressing me if I'd entertained thoughts of joining my mother anywhere in the world. Snap out of it, woman, I told myself. Hubert shouting, 'Kate! There's something wrong with Jasper!' did just that. I dashed downstairs, depression quickly replaced by sheer anxiety.

Fourteen

Hubert stood in the hall gazing forlornly at Jasper, who lay on the carpet shaking his head and then rubbing his right ear on the Axminster. Occasionally he whimpered and when I picked him up and gently looked in his ear I noticed it was obviously red and inflamed.

'The vet will sort him,' I said. 'Don't worry.'

'That's easy enough to say,' he said, still watching Jasper anxiously. 'You couldn't take him, could you?' Then he added, 'I've got an early funeral. And you're better at that sort of thing.'

'I'd agree with that,' I said. 'I'll take him straight away.'

I carried Jasper to the car and he nestled in my arms quietly, as if knowing I was only concerned with his well-being. At the Longborough Veterinary Hospital on the outskirts of town, I was first in the queue, and Jasper Humberstone and I were soon in a treatment room, where a handsome Australian vet called Mark Fairweather made a fuss of Jasper and we chatted about Oz and New Zealand and the current dramas in Longborough.

'Zoe Burrows worked here for a while,' he said. 'Just as a volunteer. She was a good worker. A natural with animals. It's a real shame.'

He began examining Jasper's chest and ears, and by now Jasper was completely in his thrall. I have to admit I was as well.

We eventually left with eardrops, antibiotics and painkillers. Plus Mark had invited me out to dinner. I played it safe by saying I'd ring him at work when I was a little less busy. 'What do you do for a living?' he asked. When I told him, he said that was 'cool'. I looked at him a little more closely and realized he was at least ten years younger than me. That disappointed me, but I was flattered and determined to take him up on his invitation.

Hubert was out on my return. I medicated Jasper and he snuggled down in his dog bed and fell instantly asleep. When the phone did ring a few minutes later, it was Hubert wanting an update on Jasper's condition. The relief in his voice was obvious, but he remained concerned and felt I shouldn't leave Jasper on his own. I wasn't particularly happy about that, but I agreed.

'On your desk, I've left you something to think about,' he said. 'Connections with Humberstone's.'

'I don't understand.'

'Neither do I, but there it is. Ivy, Alvira's husband, Zoe's grandfather, Alice, of course, and lastly Lianne Brooks.'

'Lianne?' I queried.

'I looked up Brooks in my records. We buried her grandmother three months ago.'

'In a town this size,' I said. 'You being the biggest and the best funeral director, hundreds of people will have some connection with Humberstone's.'

'That may be so, but they're all very recent.'

'What are you trying to say?' I asked.

'You're the PI, you figure it out.'

'If only I could,' I said. 'But let's face it, murder on this scale isn't normal. And a connection with Humberstone's might mean one of your staff being involved.'

'No one on my staff would...' He broke off. 'Just do your best, Kate. Do your best.'

I sat for a while in my office staring at Hubert's list. I didn't think it was either sinister or worth a follow-up. People died and got buried, either with Humberstone's or the Co-op.

Already the morning was dragging. I rang Megan but the call was short because Katy was fretful.

By twelve mid-day I decided that, as Jasper had hardly stirred, it was safe to leave him for an hour or so. I left him a few doggy chocs, slipped on my coat and crept out feeling only marginally less guilty than if I was leaving a sleeping child.

I wasn't sure if it was purely in my imagination, fuelled by gloomy grey clouds, but the town shoppers seemed tense. And although they appeared to stop and talk to each other in twos and threes more than usual, I sensed wariness and a tendency to look over their shoulders.

In the chemist, as I queued for toothpaste and soap, the usual chit-chat about the weather, the state of the roads and the vagaries of rubbish collections which passes for conversation amongst virtual strangers were replaced by dire statements – 'we're not safe anywhere these days' and 'the police don't seem to know what they're doing – do they?' There were nods all round and murmurs of agreement. Even the elderly pharmacist appeared from his inner sanctuary to say, 'Home before dark, ladies. I don't want to lose any more customers.'

I decided that I had enough time for lunch at Harry's Place, and although I was disappointed to find all the tables taken, at least the atmosphere was slightly more upbeat. I joined the queue standing behind Mr Tuna Mayonnaise. He was of average height and build, hair sparse at the back, and he held in readiness a tight little purse, which meant, in my estimation, he was either a tight wad or it was another manifestation of eccentricity.

Sal served him. 'Did you join in the search, love?' she asked him cheerfully.

'No ... I ... er ... didn't hear about it in time.'

'Don't you watch the telly?' she asked as she lathered his white bread with the tuna mayonnaise filling.

'I don't have a television. I prefer listening to music.'

'I like a bit of heavy metal,' said Sal.

'I prefer the classics,' he said, not looking at her.

'Well yeah, so do I,' said Sal, as she handed him his cellophane-wrapped sandwich. 'Nothing beats a bit of Elvis, does it?'

He muttered something I didn't catch, then shook down coins from his purse and counted out exactly the right amount of money for his lunch. Then with a 'Much obliged', he hurried out.

'Funny bugger,' said Sal, winking at me. 'Now, what can I do for you?'

'I wondered if you'd heard anything of Harry.'

She leaned towards me and whispered,

'We don't know for sure, but we think he might have gone to his sister's in Manchester. Don't say anything to the police. He needs a bit of peace and quiet.'

I nodded sagely and ordered a chicken and bacon baguette, and while Sal was making it, I asked her if she knew where Mr Tuna Mayonnaise lived. She laughed. 'His name's Scott Pelham, love. He lives near here, but I'm not sure where...'

'He lives in Carby Close,' interrupted Tone. 'He's the probate clerk at Digby and Marsh.'

'You're a fund of information you two,' I said. 'Don't suppose you know the number in Carby Close?'

Tone shook his head. 'No, 'fraid not, but I think it's an end house.'

That was better than nothing. 'Is he married?' I asked casually.

Sal laughed, 'Who'd 'ave 'im? He's polite, I'll say that for him, but he's as dull as Skegness in the middle of January.'

I heard the scraping of chairs behind me as three people decamped, and I decided to eat my baguette. I realized Hubert would be sure to know a probate man from Digby and Marsh. So, at least, I didn't have to fret any more about info on Scott Pelham. He interested me – he fitted the age group and build, he seemed to be a loner, and finally, his damning fault, he was eccentric in his habits and had no TV. Shame on you, I reprimanded myself – I was merely being prejudiced and cynical. However, in his own way, he was intriguing, and in his work on probate, his clients had all suffered a loss. Maybe there was a connection.

I finished my lunch, and went home. As I opened the door, I could hear Jasper giving a rather feeble greeting bark. I rushed upstairs to find him wagging his tail energetically. After a few minutes, he began shaking his head again but his nose was cold and he drank plenty of water. He was on the mend.

Unfortunately Hubert had phoned twice to enquire about Jasper's health. The phone rang again before I had time to be creative with my excuse for leaving a sick dog. I took a deep breath before answering, fully expecting it to be Hubert. Instead a well-modulated male voice said, 'I believe you're a private investigator?'

'Yes indeed,' I said firmly.

'My name is Graham Burrows. My daughter Zoe was found murdered. I'm sure you've heard about it.'

I paused in surprise. 'Yes ... I'm very sorry.'

'The police seem to think I killed my own daughter.'

I wasn't quite sure how to answer that appropriately, so I waited for a few moments.

'I'll say here and now – I did not kill my daughter. I only ever wanted to protect her.'

'How can I help?'

'It's obvious, isn't it? I want you to find the killer.'

'The police are doing all they can, extra staff have been drafted in. I don't see there is much I can do.'

'That's the point, isn't it? Their only suspect is me. I need you to prove it wasn't me.'

'You may have been questioned, Mr Burrows, but you haven't been charged. Presumably because you're innocent.'

'Of course I'm innocent...' He broke off. 'Would a reward make a difference?'

'Who to?'

'The someone who knows who the killer is. He must have friends and relatives.'

'I think the police would want a say in reward-offering.'

'The chief inspector who interviewed me only seemed concerned with finding me guilty. You'd think, now that another girl has gone missing, they'd leave me alone.'

I paused for a moment to think. I didn't want to get involved. 'I still don't know how I can help you.'

'Well, for goodness' sake,' he blustered. 'Do what you're supposed to do – snoop.'

I didn't like his tone, but I said calmly

enough, 'Before I do that, we'll have to meet and discuss my involvement – if any.'

'My only requirement,' he snapped, 'is that you get the police off my back and find the killer.'

That's a bloody tall order, I muttered to myself. Already I disliked him, and wondered if Waterworth did too, and that was why he had him firmly in his sights. Or, of course, there may have been some circumstantial evidence I knew nothing about.

'I'll check my diary,' I said. I flicked through the empty pages. 'Would eleven thirty tomorrow morning suit you?'

'Fine,' he said. 'I'm on compassionate leave.' He followed that with a grudging thank you.

'One more thing,' I said. 'Did Zoe have a boyfriend?'

'She was far too young.'

I tried not to be prejudiced against him. He was after all a grieving father with the additional burden of being a suspect, but even so, I had a strong suspicion we were not going to get on. I needed to talk to Hubert, partly because I really didn't want to take on Graham Burrows as a client and I needed to be told I was making the right decision.

My confidence as a PI was already at an all-time low. In fact, just lately I couldn't resist either the lonely-hearts column or the jobs section of the local paper. I kidded myself that I was looking for a woman for Hubert in the lonely hearts, but I couldn't use that excuse for my job search.

When Hubert finally returned that evening, he'd bought a bag of dog treats for Jasper and a scowl for me for leaving Jasper alone for little more than an hour. Jasper's medicaments had improved his condition already, and Hubert mellowed towards me as the evening progressed. So much so that when I told him about the request from Graham Burrows, he guessed I didn't want to take on the case.

'Perhaps you're suffering from burnout,' he said as he settled Jasper beside him on the sofa. 'I'm sure it happens to PIs.'

If Hubert had told me that in the past, I would have snapped his head off. Now I merely shrugged and murmured lamely, 'I need to pay the rent.'

'It doesn't worry me if you pay the rent.'

'It worries me.'

'If you don't want to take up the Burrows case – don't. It's as simple as that.'

Hubert closed his eyes and began to doze. I watched him for some time. We *were* like an old married couple, and I was scared. I needed to make plans for a future that didn't include Hubert.

Towards the end of *News at Ten*, Hubert

stirred just in time to hear that there had been two sightings of Lianne Brooks which the police were feeling optimistic about.

'That ends the day on a better note,' said Hubert, pouring himself a nightcap. 'And if you decide to pack up the agency, you could always work for me.'

It took a few moments for me to answer. 'You're either born to a life of undertaking or you're not. And believe me, Hubert – I was not.'

He had to have the last word. 'Sleep on it,' he said. 'You might change your mind.'

On my way to bed, I muttered to myself, 'Not if I slept for a hundred years, mate!'

Fifteen

Graham Burrows arrived to the minute. A dapper little man wearing a fawn trench coat and cap, he reminded me of an elderly jockey. His thin face and small features had not been reproduced in the photos I'd seen of Zoe. He held out his small hand to shake mine, and its warmth and softness reminded me of a child's. It felt strangely repulsive.

Even before we'd sat down in my office, he was trying to take charge. 'Now then,' he said. 'Where do we start?'

'I start by asking you to tell me why the police suspect you. And before you answer, I'm undecided about taking on your case.'

'Just tell me how much you want,' he said nastily. 'I'll pay anything.'

'It's not a question of money, Mr Burrows, so let us both stay calm, shall we?'

His expression showed he didn't appreciate my patronizing tone, but he mumbled, 'I've been under a lot of strain.'

'Yes, of course you have.'

I opened my notebook and raised my pen

161

in a businesslike fashion. 'Have the police given you a reason for their suspicions?'

He shrugged. 'They kept asking about *men* in her life. But she was only a girl. I know she had one or two crushes on boys at school, but we kept a close eye on her.'

'Did you lose your temper?'

'When?'

'With the police,' I said innocently.

'I got a bit rattled. Anyone would. I'm being used as a...' He struggled for the word.

'Fall guy?' I suggested.

'Precisely.'

'Tell me about Zoe,' I said quietly.

He swallowed hard. 'She was as good as gold until she was fifteen. She went to church on Sunday and to the church youth club on a Wednesday evening. Then suddenly she changed.'

'Do you know why?'

'Oh yes. She got mixed up with a rough crowd at school, and that was when she became ... difficult.'

'In what way?'

His head dropped a little to one side, making him look sly, but his answer was straightforward enough, 'She'd always been fastidiously tidy about everything. Then she stopped tidying her room. She was rude, aggressive and demanding to both me and her mother.'

'Drugs? Staying out late? Trouble with the police?'

'Certainly not!'

'So far, Mr Burrows, your daughter's behaviour sounds perfectly normal for an adolescent girl. Did she tell you what time she'd be in at night?'

'I told her. I wanted her home no later than ten p.m.'

'A bit unrealistic for an eighteen-year-old.'

He thought about that for a moment and twisted his wedding band around. 'We cared about her. I wanted to keep her safe. Children of that age need protecting from themselves.'

'Zoe wasn't a child any more – that's the point. She was a woman.'

I supposed that intellectually he knew that, but emotionally he hadn't come to terms with her being an adult. And sadly now he never could.

His shoulders slumped and his eyes glistened. I still didn't like him, but I did feel sorry for him. He was the sort of man who wouldn't cry openly but inside his heart was breaking. So far there had been no mention of religion and I felt he was holding back on that in the same way he was holding back the tears. 'She was my child,' he said brokenly. 'I wanted to protect her all her life ... now we can't even bury her.'

'That time will come,' I said.

There was a long pause before he murmured, 'My Zoe will be safe in heaven.'

'That thought will always be a comfort to you,' I said. I believed in neither heaven nor hell, but I did believe in everlasting peace.

'I'm a religious man,' he said dully. 'Or at least I try to be. You'd think that would make me a better person. The police don't think so. They think I'm a crank. They're taught to be politically correct towards other religions, but when it comes to Christianity, they think they can disparage my beliefs.'

'Perhaps the police think you lost your temper with Zoe because she couldn't live up to your religious ideals.'

'Well, I didn't,' he snapped. 'I accepted that she didn't want to go to church any more. I just hoped that she...'He broke off. 'Her mother's lost her faith ... have you any idea how hard it is to hang on to your faith?'

I shook my head. He stared at me with his pale sad eyes for several seconds and then said quietly, 'Zoe was not my natural daughter. Not my DNA. I haven't told the police, although they'll find out soon enough, and when they do, I suppose they'll think that was a reason to kill her.'

'Was she adopted?'

'No. Her mother, Tina, was seventeen and pregnant when I met her. I was twenty. We

164

fell in love and I decided that the child would be mine in all but genes. Zoe was a lovely child. And I swear to God that I did not murder her.'

I wondered why there hadn't been more children, maybe they chose not to, or he was gay or sterile. Not that it mattered, because I believed he hadn't killed Zoe.

'I believe you,' I said. 'But I'm only willing to take on the case unpaid and on a casual basis. If I do find anything out, I'll be reporting it to the police.'

He didn't look pleased. 'It's better than nothing.'

It was time to discuss tactics. Not that mine would be different. 'I want you to detail the last week of Zoe's life. What she did, what time she came in, what was her mood like? Did she make any calls? Use the Internet? Anything you can think of. Can you do that?'

'Of course.'

'Good. I know you'll be meticulous. Once I have that information, I'll have something to work on.'

He stood up to leave and murmured, 'Thank you.'

'You may find that you didn't know your daughter as well as you thought. Be prepared for that.'

He smiled bleakly. I took him down to the

front door and watched as he walked away. A sad little man whose beliefs had been shaken and his world torn apart by a killer who might be someone he knew. It crossed my mind that on Sunday he might be eyeing the congregation with suspicion. Just as I glanced at perfectly ordinary-looking men in the street and wondered – is it you?

Sixteen

Jade's tip-off about Zoe seeing a man called Stewart Walker needed following up, and proved easy enough. I found him in the telephone directory.

Hubert was occupied that morning and had walked Jasper early, so at ten a.m. I decided that a visit to Walker and Mr Tuna Mayonnaise, aka Scott Pelham, was to be a priority for the day.

I parked my car outside Walker's house in Goren Close, part of a small estate of new detached houses. I sat with a map in my hands and wondered exactly what Jade had meant by an 'older' guy. When I was a teen-ager, 'older' was twenty-two – 'old' was thirty-five, 'elderly' was past forty, and any ideas of sex with a man that age were virtual necrophilia. The houses surrounding me in the cul-de-sac would cost upwards of £250,000. They had double garages and one or two had electronic gates. Newspapers had recently told us the average age for first-time buyers was thirty-four. It seemed even more likely that Stewart Walker was an 'older' man, for few first-time buyers could afford to live in Goren Close.

There was no one about and no sign of life in the house. Patience not being a virtue of mine, although I was trying to cultivate it, meant that, after an hour of ruining my teeth with half a packet of Polos, I decided to come back later. Expensive houses meant working long hours, and I guessed Walker wouldn't be home much before eight. I was just about to give up when I saw movement at the window. A woman holding a baby. She was patting his back and talking and smiling. You bastard, Walker!

At just after twelve mid-day, I walked to Harry's Place. Harry's absence seemed to have made no difference to trade, and Tone and Sal had a queue of four, and two tables occupied. They both gave me a friendly wave as I sat down at a table by the window. A few minutes later, Sal came up to take my order.

'Any news of Harry?' I asked.

'Not yet,' she said as she wiped over my perfectly clean table. 'I hope he hasn't done anything daft.'

'At least the police have caught the arsonist.'

'Have they?' queried Sal.

'Yes. It seems it was Alice's son.'

I knew by the expression on her face that

she'd known all along that Alice had a son. She sat down beside me and, in a voice barely above a whisper, said, 'It's no good being secretive now, is it – I mean, we kept quiet to protect her. She only came back to Longborough because she thought that was the last place he'd look for her.'

'What was his grievance?' I asked.

She shrugged. 'I dunno. Stark raving he was, especially when he didn't take his medication. The doctors said he wasn't a danger to anyone except his mother. For years he'd been threatening her, calling her the "whore of Babylon", whatever that means. If he beat her up, they took him away, and he was in various mental hospitals. Each time Alice moved, he seemed to find her. Then she met Harry and he told her to stop running and he'd protect her. It's made it so much worse for him that he couldn't manage to do that.'

'Surely her own son didn't rape her?' I asked. Not that I thought that was likely, but I wanted to see Sal's reaction.

'No,' she said. 'That was someone else.'

Her reply was a bit too swift. 'How do you know?' I asked.

'Well, she said it wasn't him. She said she'd have known her own son, even covered from head to toe in a bin liner.'

There was no arguing with that, so I changed tack. 'What about his father?'

169

'Alice never mentioned him. One-night stand when she was young – it happens.'

I saw him then from the corner of my eye – Mr Tuna Mayonnaise. Sal saw me watching him. Once he'd stood at the counter, I said, 'You know about people, Sal. Does he give you the creeps?'

She thought for a moment. 'No – not really. We have so many odd-bods in here. He's no more odd than most, except for always having the same thing. There's no law against it.'

Sal left then to help Tone, and as Mr Tuna Mayonnaise, a.k.a. Scott Pelham, left, I way-laid him. 'I'm sorry to bother you,' I said as I flipped open my notebook. 'I'm research-ing lunch-time eating habits and I wondered if you could spare a minute or two.'

'I am meant to be at work,' he said. 'But I could spare a minute.'

'I have noticed that you always have a tuna mayo sandwich.'

'You're very observant,' he said with a wry smile. 'But actually I don't eat lunch.'

My surprise was obvious.

'You should be talking to my girlfriend,' he said. 'She's obsessive about eating the same things every day. Shredded wheat for breakfast, tuna mayo for lunch and a chicken salad in the evening. I've tried to make her see sense, but she won't change. It's embarrassing, but I just have to grin and bear it. She's a lovely girl and it's her only ... aberration. We're getting married next year, so maybe she'll change.'

He left then. I'd got him totally wrong. Far from being a sinister loner, he was a besotted fiancé and he saved her shoe leather by collecting her lunch.

My confidence had reached an all time low, and only Tone turning up with my baguette stopped me from dwelling on my deficiencies.

'You're looking lovely today,' he said, smiling.

'And I thought I just looked away with the fairies.'

'You've had a near-death experience,' he said. 'Bound to make you thoughtful.'

'Did you know about Alice's son?' I asked.

He nodded. 'Yeah, but I hadn't known long. It's a shame. Only child, that was his problem. I reckon lone kids are more likely to get depressed than those who have brothers and sisters.'

'I didn't know that,' I said. 'But he wasn't just depressed, was he? He was psychotic.'

'Well – what does that mean?' said Tone with a shrug. 'He had some funny ideas. I'm just glad I've got a brother and sister.'

He walked away then with, 'Ta-ra, Kate. Keep smiling.'

I ate my lunch slowly, watching the comings and goings in the café. Now that Mr Tuna Mayonnaise had been eliminated as a sinister loner, I had one suspect less now, and Alice's murder appeared to be solved. That just left the rapes of three old ladies, the murder of Zoe and the disappearance of Lianne. In one town, that was more than a crimewave, it was a severe epidemic. And I didn't want to believe that more than one man could be involved.

Back at Humberstone's, there were three messages for me. One was from David, telling me that Charlie Dawes had confessed to his mother's murder. The next was from Zoe's father, saying he no longer wanted any input from me. The third was from Annie the carer, saying she had something to tell me.

The call that worried me the most was from Zoe's father. Having persuaded me to make inquiries, albeit on a casual basis, he'd now changed his mind. Not that I'd managed to achieve much so far, but it was still very odd.

I didn't bother to ring him back. I walked Jasper around the houses and then left him with a bowl of food and walked on my own the short distance to Chorley Avenue. It felt strange walking without him. I felt like a mother who no longer needs to push her child in a pushchair – bereft. I rang the door-bell and waited and waited.

Finally the front door opened a fraction. It was Mrs Burrows. I introduced myself and asked if her husband was in. 'He's in,' she said dully. She was a small woman, about five feet tall, with dark hair that hung limply and greyish skin. Her eyes were deeply sunken from lack of sleep, or too much drug-induced sleep. Either way she looked ill. She wore a blue towelling housecoat and slippers and I got the impression she'd just left her bed.

'Who's that?' shouted a male voice, instantly recognizable as irritable husband. He appeared then, fully dressed. 'Go back to bed, Tina,' he said gently. She turned to go, but I wanted to ask my question with no preamble. 'Mrs Burrows, did you know Zoe had an older boyfriend?'

She spun round. 'It's a lie ... a wicked rumour. She was a virgin when she died ... she was.'

'Go to bed, dear.'

'No! I won't. I want to put the record straight.' Tina Burrows' voice verged on hysteria, but Graham Burrows had paled and he began edging me away from the door. 'I want to speak ... I will speak.' Her voice was so loud now that he looked outwards towards the road, obviously scared the neighbours would hear. He pulled me into the house. 'For goodness' sake,' he said to his wife. 'Shut up!' For a moment there was silence, but the atmosphere was as brittle as footsteps on dry twigs. Tina looked at me, eyes bright with bitterness and tears. 'Find him!' she spat out. 'Just find him.' She turned then and walked away. We stood listening as she stumbled upstairs sobbing.

'She's on the edge,' Burrows said. 'And I can't bring her back.'

I muttered something about it being early days, and anger being a stage of grief. I didn't mention Stewart Walker by name. Tina's reaction and tone of voice had suggested to me she'd stop at nothing to avenge her daughter. Usually it was the father of a murdered daughter who had revenge in his heart, but my ex-client seemed strangely calm.

'I think you ought to go to her,' I said. 'The police are making progress, I'm sure. An arrest can't be far off.'

His expression was one of disbelief, but he showed me the door and apologized for wasting my time.

As I walked away, I stared at the garden shed where Zoe was killed. It seemed a flimsy affair. Had she been dragged there kicking and screaming, and if so, why had the neighbours heard nothing? Once inside, why hadn't she put up a fight and done some damage to the shed? I couldn't see from the pavement if it was padlocked. Curiosity got the better of me. I looked up at the bedroom windows. The curtains were pulled and nothing twitched other than my nerves. If they did look out, they could easily see me, I thought. And then the thought repeated itself, so that I could no longer resist looking at the murder scene.

I opened the door with a key that sat invitingly in the lock. I removed it and slipped it into my pocket. Being locked in confined spaces had happened once too often to risk it happening again. Quickly I closed the door behind me. I knew Zoe had been battered to death with a spade. Obviously the murder weapon had been taken away as evidence.

I looked around and at first glance it seemed an ordinary, shabby, earthy-smelling garden shed. A closer look, though, showed flooring that was an old but decent carpet. There was a garden chair in one corner, complete with cushions and two folded car rugs. On the shelves were empty plastic plant pots and several cans of paint. A rotary lawn-mower stood in another corner. I looked down at the floor. Plenty of space. There was lighting and red checked curtains at the small window. I jumped to a conclusion based on instinct and the atmosphere of the place. I was convinced that this was Zoe's love nest. Where else could she go? Where else could Walker go?

I was about to leave when I heard footsteps. I stood against the door and held my breath as they came closer and then stopped.

Seventeen

It seemed an age before I heard Tina Burrows shout, 'The key's gone.' I heard her retreating and very gingerly I opened the shed door. It was all clear. She'd evidently gone back into the house. I dropped the key on the ground, closed the door and then ran like hell.

Back at Humberstone's, Hubert was catching up on paperwork, but he decided to come upstairs for coffee, and as we sat at the kitchen table, I told him about the Burrowses and Stewart Walker.

'So, you're going to tell David about him?' he asked somewhat suspiciously.

'Well yes. When I've had a chance to speak to Walker.'

'If he is the murderer, what was his motive?' Hubert's tone of voice was sceptical, and I felt a warning coming on.

'It's only a guess,' I said, 'but I think they used the shed as a love nest and Zoe began to get possessive and wanted a bit more than a quickie on a hard floor and threatened to tell his wife.'

Hubert sipped at his coffee thoughtfully. 'Bit dodgy then, killing her there.'

'A spontaneous act due to fear,' I suggested.

'Why haven't the police caught up with him yet?' asked Hubert with one of his self-satisfied smiles.

'Perhaps only Jade knew about the affair.'

'Strange they weren't seen.'

I didn't comment on that. It was something that had been troubling me. Now that I'd met Tina Burrows, Stewart Walker wasn't the only suspect. But I had to see him to rule him out.

'I'm thinking of going to his place tonight,' I said.

'Not on your own you're not,' said Hubert. 'I'll come with you.'

I didn't argue. The confrontation could turn nasty, and if he was merely an adulterer, maybe it could be kept from his wife. She was after all in a very vulnerable position with a young baby to care for.

Hubert finished his coffee and returned to his paperwork. I sat for a while staring at my notebook. Seeing the name Annie reminded me I hadn't spoken to her. I rang her immediately.

'It may not be important,' she said. But I've remembered something Ivy once told me. She'd worked on a farm years ago, just

178

for a few months.'

'She didn't say exactly when or where?'

'She mentioned a place called Kingsfield. Then she laughed, but right sarcastic. Like she didn't think it was funny at all. I didn't take much notice at the time, and we didn't talk about it again. But now I just wondered...'

'Thanks, Annie. It's a sort of lead, I'm sure. I'll let you know.'

'Promise?'

'I promise.'

I wrote 'Kingsfield' in my notebook and rang the one woman who might recognize the name – Betty.

When I mentioned Kingsfield, I heard her gasp. 'You've given me a turn, you 'ave,' she said. 'A real turn. I shall 'ave to sit down.' I expected her to rally quickly but there was only silence. 'Betty, are you all right?'

'Yeah. I'm OK now. Just a shock to hear that name again.' Her voice sounded weary.

'Is it a village?' I asked.

'No, love. It's a farm, or it was a farm. I should think it's derelict after all these years. I should leave well alone.'

'Why's that?' I asked, trying to sound casual.

'Water under the bridge, dear. Best left.'

'Can I come to see you?'

Betty hesitated. 'I'll 'ave to think about

that. I'm feeling a bit tired. Tell you what – I'll ring you.'

As the phone went dead, I sat staring at it. Far from dulling my interest in Kingsfield, it had of course heightened it. I rang Megan's number to put the same question to Alvira, but there was no reply, so I left a message on the answerphone.

Later that evening, I told Hubert about Kingsfield. He'd never heard the name. 'I reckon you're going off at a tangent,' he said. 'You just concentrate on one thing at a time. Walker is your priority at the moment.' Then he added, 'Anyway, this isn't a proper case. Burrows has dropped you, and at this rate you won't be able to pay your rent.'

'Throw me out on to the streets then,' I snapped.

'Don't tempt me,' said Hubert.

I think he was joking.

We left for Goren Close just before eight. It was pouring with rain and Hubert insisted on bringing his huge black umbrella. In a black mac with a hood, I couldn't make up my mind if he looked like a flasher or an old-style East End gangster, but if I saw him dressed like that at my front door on a dark and rainy night, I'd have been worried.

Walker, definitely an older man, probably in his forties, was good-looking in a tanned suave way. He wore tight jeans over a tight bum, and a navy sweater that clung to his well-developed pecs. He wasn't worried at first, he simply queried, 'Jehovah's Witnesses?'

I went for the shock tactic. 'No – murder investigators.'

His mouth dropped open. 'What are you talking about?'

'The death of Zoe Burrows.'

'Oh my God! You can't come in.'

'You have some questions to answer,' I said. 'We don't care where.'

His eyes darted between the two of us. Hubert the silent stared at him menacingly.

'In the garage. I'm selling a car. I'll tell my wife that's why you're here.'

He left us standing in the porch while he closed the door on us and went inside to lie to his wife yet again.

'That was easy,' I said. 'He didn't even ask who we were.'

Hubert muttered something about not counting chickens, and after standing there for several minutes, I was beginning to feel that he was right. Perhaps Walker had already done a runner via his back door.

Eventually, though, he reappeared and muttered that the baby wasn't well. He opened one of the two garages with an electronic keypad. Inside sat a blue Honda car. Hubert couldn't resist having a look at it. 'It's a bargain,' said Walker. 'My wife doesn't want to drive any more – she wants me to sell it. There's nothing wrong with it – only twelve thousand on the clock.'

'Zoe Burrows!' I said sharply.

'I didn't kill her. I hardly knew her.'

'But you were shagging her in the garden shed.'

'How did you know that?'

'I'm gifted. And in my gifted eye I saw her begging you to leave your wife. Making threats – saying she would tell your wife. You'd promised to leave your wife, hadn't you? But there was always an excuse. The little trollop had you by the balls and you saw the red mist – picked up the spade and battered her to death.'

He began shaking his head. 'No, no, no! You're not gifted. You're deluded. Zoe wasn't a trollop. Zoe was a lovely girl. I was mad about her...'

'Not mad at her?'

'You have got it so wrong!' he snapped. 'Zoe wanted the excitement of an affair, but she didn't want a relationship. She wanted to leave Longborough and travel and have plenty of fun before she settled down. If I'd left my wife, she wouldn't have seen me again.'

I must have looked unconvinced, because even more emphatically he said, 'Zoe met me in secret. We made love. I adored her. And, to be honest, I would have given up everything to be with her. But she wanted to be a free spirit and I just lived in hope that one day she would feel the same way about me.'

'So what happened the night she died?' I asked.

He rested his hand on the bonnet of the car and frowned. 'I really don't know. I'd left the house saying I was having a quick drink with a friend, and she was already waiting for me in the shed. We didn't put on the light, and I was only with her for about half an hour. She seemed very tired and I assumed that she'd go into the house as soon as I'd left...' He broke off. 'Zoe was alive when I left her.'

'So that suggests,' I said, 'a homicidal maniac just happened to be passing by and found her by chance.'

Hubert nudged me then, noticing that Walker's face had become ashen. The hand on the car bonnet was now an arm as he tried to support himself. 'Don't you dare pass out,' I said. 'You've got to go back in the house and tell a pack of lies to your wife – "It was a passing fling ... she did all the running ... you were weak ... you felt left out because of the baby."'

'I know I've been a bastard, but you don't

understand...'

'No, and neither will she. You've wrecked two families because your brain was in your trousers.'

Perhaps I should have been more sympathetic but I wasn't. He was no lovestruck teenager. He was supposed to be mature, a family man. But, weak and disloyal though he was, I didn't think he was Zoe's killer.

'What about Zoe's father?' I asked.

'What about him?'

'Was she afraid of him?'

He looked puzzled. 'No. But she was scared of her mum.'

At that moment a high-pitched hysterical voice called out, 'Stewart! Stewart, I need some help.'

Stewart righted himself and took a deep breath. 'My wife does not cope well with anything.' Then he added under his breath, 'If I was going to kill anyone, it would be her.'

'You'd better go,' I said. 'The police will be in touch, but I don't think you'll be chief suspect.'

'Sometimes I think a real prison would be a welcome change,' he said bitterly. As he spoke, his wife screamed out his name in competition with the equally distressed screams of their baby. He was rushing away when he turned. 'Who the hell are you anyway?'

I didn't answer. Stewart Walker was off my list as a murder suspect, but I didn't think he was the type to learn any lessons. Another young woman would come along and he'd think himself 'in love' for a few months until the excitement wore off. Years down the line he'd get more pathetic and he'd still be with his wife.

In the car, as the rain thrashed against the windscreen, Hubert's thoughts reflected my own. 'Sad bastard!' Then he added, 'Do you think Zoe's mother killed her?'

'I do. I think she saw him leave the shed from the bedroom window. So she came downstairs to confront her daughter and maybe Zoe got abusive and Tina picked up the spade and battered her with it.'

'What are you going to do about it?'

'I'm going to tell David about Walker and my suspicions.'

'So you don't want to do anything about it yourself?' he whispered.

'I can hear you,' I said. 'But no. This case is not for mere amateurs. And I'm getting older and wiser.'

'What does that make me?' asked Hubert, sounding slightly perturbed.

'That makes you a cross between Methuselah and Solomon.'

'I really do feel my age now. Thanks, Kate.'

We drove off, but after a few yards I said, 'Drop me off in Station Road, will you? I want to talk to Betty a bit more about Kingsfield.'

'I'll wait in the car for you.'

'There's no need...' I began, then added hastily. 'Thanks, Hubert.' I was thinking more of the rain and getting wet than any danger.

We were driving slowly past the station towards Betty's house when I saw a sight that disturbed me. A middle-aged man stood hatless in the pouring rain. He was talking into a mobile phone and in his other hand he held another mobile phone. His body language said it all. Something awful had happened.

'Stop the car,' I said. 'That man's in trouble.'

'How the hell do you know that?'

'Look at him. He looks demented.'

He stopped the car. 'He could be on drink or drugs or just raving.'

'Well, I'm going to find out.'

Hubert followed me reluctantly, brolly up and a nervous look on his face.

As I approached the man, I could hear him shouting into the phone. 'You've got to do something ... I don't know what to do...' He broke off when he saw me. 'For God's sake!' he cried out. 'Won't someone help me?'

Eighteen

The agitated man wore a grey anorak and grey trousers that clung wetly to his legs. What remained of his hair hung in strands, but it was his eyes, in the street lights, that were his most notable feature. They were frightened, anxious, even desperate.

'What's happened?' I asked.

'It's my wife – she's been taken. She's disappeared,' he said as he frantically looked around. 'I've rung the police and they say she must have wandered off. They think we're both senile. If she was eighteen, they'd be out looking for her ... wouldn't they...? Just as they're doing for that Lianne girl – well, wouldn't they?'

'I think, sir,' said Hubert quietly. 'You need to be out of the rain. Come and sit in my car and tell us what's happening.'

'I can't. I can't. She might come back.'

Hubert pointed to the car and said, 'We can see her easily from the car. It gives a good view of the station.'

'Who are you?' he asked as he thrust the

two mobile phones into his anorak pocket.

'I'm Hubert Humberstone, a local businessman, and this is Kate – she's a private investigator.'

I was glad Hubert didn't elaborate, because it might have seemed to the stranger that we were touting for customers.

'I'm Frank Pattingham,' he murmured. He began to shiver and he looked across at the car and said wearily, 'All right, I'll sit in your car for a while and I'll ring the police again.'

'I'll do that for you,' I said. 'As soon as you tell us what's happened.'

Once in the car, Hubert surprised me by taking a hip flask from the glove compartment and offering it to Frank. He didn't take any persuading and took two huge slugs. Once Frank had stopped shivering, he started talking. 'She's disappeared into thin air, I'm telling you ... no one saw anything ... it's my fault I arrived late ... the train came in early...' I put my hand up to stop him. 'Could we start at the beginning, Mr Pattingham. What's your wife's name?

'Grace.'

'And you came to meet her off the train?'

'Yes. Every week she goes to see her sister in Birmingham and I meet the train at eight fifteen. I was a bit late and the train was five minutes early...' He broke off and took another swallow of brandy from the flask. 'If

188

only the train hadn't been early.'

'You're sure she was on the train?'

'Of course I'm sure. She rang me an hour before the train was due in. She didn't realize it was running five minutes early.'

'And she wasn't in the waiting room or the ticket hall?'

He flashed me an exasperated look. 'I've looked everywhere. In the Ladies. On all the platforms. For God's sake, I even checked the tracks. No sign except this.' From his pocket he withdrew the mobile phone.

'Where did you find it?' asked Hubert.

Frank pointed to a patch of grass just outside the station. I dug into the dark reaches of my coat pocket and found a thin polythene bag saved from a supermarket trip. I asked Frank to let me have the mobile phone so that the police could check for fingerprints.

'They're not interested,' he said bitterly. 'When I said Grace was sixty-five years old, they asked if she was "well". I told them she was fit and active, but then this bright spark of a duty sergeant suggested she might be confused. Had we just moved? Had she been under stress lately? Were there any problems in the family? Questions – bloody questions. If they got off their backsides, they might find her before it's too late.'

He began to weep silently then. A few tears

only, but his body was racked by them. It was Hubert who put an arm round him. I used my mobile to ring David. With no pre-amble, I said, 'A woman has been abducted from the train station – we need help.'

'Why the hell are you involved?'

'Divine intervention. Will you come, please...? Please?'

'I'm on my way.'

While we waited for him, Frank showed me the photo he kept of Grace in his wallet. She was standing at her front door with a kitten in her arms. Grace was slim, with salt and pepper short hair, wearing flat shoes, a brown skirt, white blouse and a beige cardigan. 'Taken in the summer, that was,' he said. 'Just after we bought Daisy – the cat.'

Grace looked every inch the sensible, reliable old school health visitor. Not the type to run off or bring attention to herself.

David arrived within ten minutes, so he'd had enough time to check out the initial call. Thankfully I hadn't lied and said she was a teenager. He parked his car behind us and said he wanted to talk to Frank alone. We could sit in his car.

Hubert and I slunk into the back of David's car and waited and waited.

Eventually he braved the rain to tell us the search would start at first light, and in the meantime the station would be cordoned off and a PC would stand guard and also check to see if the cameras had picked up anything.

'I'll take Frank home,' he said. 'He's sent for his daughter – she should be there by now. You two can make tracks. I'll ring you later, Kate.'

I wasn't one bit happy, but we swopped cars again and Frank managed a sad little wave as he was driven off.

Hubert switched on the car engine for warmth. 'What do you make of Grace going missing?'

'What do you mean?' I asked.

'Wife, fed up with retirement, decides to disappear,' said Hubert. 'It happens. Or she's been kidnapped.'

'Kidnaps happen,' I agreed. But he didn't exactly give me the impression of having much to offer in the way of ransom money.'

'You didn't recognize the name then?'

'No, why should I?'

'Big lottery winner last year.'

'Well, he hasn't let it go to his head, has he?'

'Meow,' said Hubert.

'Sorry, but I think the rapist has targeted another victim.'

'You can't be sure.'

'Of course not, but I refuse to believe Longborough could produce, in one winter,

191

two murderers, one serial rapist of old ladies, plus a kidnapper. It doesn't seem feasible to me.'

'We'll see,' said Hubert. 'When the ransom note comes.'

I left it at that and decided that I'd visit Betty in the morning. Hubert had worked all day, and Betty could talk for hours, so it would have to wait.

Once indoors, we both had hot baths and Hubert made cocoa and began grilling bacon for sandwiches. We sat watching the TV on the sofa with Jasper splayed between us, in our dressing gowns, half expecting news of Grace Pattingham's abduction, but there was none.

'What makes you so sure Grace is a victim of the rapist?' asked Hubert. 'And, unless he's left her for dead, what would he do with her?'

'Perhaps he took too many risks. Betty reported her rape and she makes a good witness. Knowing that, he decides inside jobs are too risky. He doesn't want to get caught, so his best bet is to take a woman off the street – an older woman.' I paused. 'Like the other women – someone he knew. Someone who knew him. My bet is Grace trusted this man. Maybe he had a chat with her. Perhaps he was on the same train.'

'You're just guessing, Kate. Let the police

handle it.'

'No. They concentrate on known sex offenders and they don't seem to have a single suspect. This man is new to it. Something has triggered him off.'

'Like what?' asked Hubert as he slurped his cocoa.

'You tell me.'

'OK – drink, drugs, bereavement, being jilted at the altar, his dog died, he stopped taking his medication – take your choice, Kate.'

'You've got no trust in my judgement at all, have you?'

'I do,' he said. 'But you don't have any evidence and not one single suspect.'

He was right, of course. But the bastard was out there stalking elderly women. He threatened to kill, but killing wasn't on his agenda. Had he chosen Grace because he wanted her for his own? Not just a lock of hair, but the whole package. A human trophy. For the ultimate lonely loner. An older woman who, in his demented imagination, will ... nurture him like a Gran? Far more likely was that the rapes were some sort of revenge for past slights or emotional trauma.

My thoughts were interrupted by the phone. It was David. He sounded angry.

'Waterworth wants a low-key search. He

says if and when we get a ransom note we'll pull out all the stops. He wants a news blackout, but how the hell he thinks a search can take place in secret is beyond me. Meanwhile, Frank has rung dozens of people, so by now all of Longborough knows anyway.'

'You need a cuddle,' I said.

He managed a brief laugh. 'I need more than that.'

There was a hint of suggestion in his voice, but I wanted to talk about Kingsfield, wherever that was. Anyway, someone called him and he said, 'I must go. By the way, Grace worked as a health visitor in Longborough for twenty years. She must have known quite a few people.'

The next morning, in mere light drizzle, I walked to Station Road. There was a PC with a notepad standing by a sandwich board on which there was a photo of Grace and the caption: 'HAVE YOU SEEN THIS WOMAN?' He appeared to be stopping people, although several of them, rushing for trains, avoided him.

The PC was young, good-looking, and wore rimless glasses which made him look studious. I told him I was a friend of DI Todman and that I was a PI and a friend of Grace Pattingham. He stared at me for a moment. 'Name?' I told him. 'Were you on the train arriving at ten past eight last night?' I shook my head. 'Were you in the station or surrounding area between eight and eight thirty p.m.?'

'No ... but.'

'Thank you for your time, madam.' I was left open-mouthed as a couple approached and he asked them to look at the poster. I just knew from his accent and his arrogance what he was. 'Fast-tracker!' I muttered as I hurried away.

I was a little put out, and even more so when, just as I arrived at Betty's house, carer Annie was leaving. 'What's going on?' I asked.

'Hi, Kate,' said Annie, with a worried frown. 'Betty's had a heart attack. She's refusing to go into hospital. The district nurse and I were meant to meet here to assess her needs, but she's been delayed. We're going to meet up at twelve.'

'How is she?'

'She's in bed. She's a bit confused and rambling, but not confused enough to refuse hospital. Says she wants to die in her own bed – which is fair enough, isn't it?'

'Sure. It's what I'd want.'

We chatted for a while about the baby, and then I asked, 'Is Betty well enough for visitors?'

'She is, but she says she wants a good long

nap now, so it might be best to come back later.'

'I'll come back just after twelve.'

Annie drove away and I decided to walk to the florist's to buy Betty some flowers. On the way, I even peered in at the Co-op funeral director's, but the waiting room was full, so I decided against seeing Daphne again. She hadn't been helpful the first time, so she was unlikely to help me this time. I bought Betty a large and cheery mixed bouquet, and then made my way to the town's newspaper office. It was in the obituary notices I convinced myself I would find a clue. A fairly recent death or an anniversary of a sudden and tragic death might well send someone over the edge.

The staff were helpful, everything was on computer, but I sat for over two hours reading death notices, poems for beloved Grans and Granddads, and the prayers for the occasional tragic death of a child or young person. It made depressing reading and I was ready to give up when one caught my eye – 'In remembrance of our long-suffering mother Freda. Still missed but always in our thoughts and deeds. From her children.'

No surname, no dates – which made me interested rather than suspicious. 'Long-suffering' implied it had been a protracted finale, and the name Freda suggested she was elderly. At least I had a first name, so it was worth checking out at the Co-op. The acknowledgement was six months old.

The Co-op funeral parlour would have to wait. It was ten past twelve and my chance to see Betty. There were two cars parked outside, and I hung around for a while until I started to feel conspicuous. I knocked on the door, to be greeted by an ageing district nurse with grey hair scraped back into a tight bun. At first her face looked as tight as her bun, but when she smiled, her face was transformed. She ushered me in. 'We're having a cup of tea with Betty – come and join us.'

Upstairs, Betty was propped up in bed against white pillows. Her cheeks had an unhealthy flush, but she seemed cheerful enough and she remembered me. 'I'm glad you've come...' Then, spying my flowers, she beamed with delight. 'Lovely flowers,' she said. 'I haven't had fresh flowers in ages and ages. You'll find a vase under the kitchen sink.'

The district nurse followed me downstairs. 'Betty's very poorly. Her GP doesn't think she's got long. She's adamant she won't go into hospital. I just wondered...' She paused. 'I know it's a cheek, but you are an ex-nurse – you couldn't pop back early evening and give her a drink and some sandwiches ... could you? We've got two mobile carers off sick. They should be back soon.'

'I'll come about six,' I said, not feeling I had much choice. 'Have the overnight visits been arranged?'

As I searched for the vase in the over-crowded cupboard under the sink, the district nurse, who'd now introduced herself as Linda Parks, said, 'Her nephew is coming about midnight – says he'll stay over at night for the foreseeable.'

Back upstairs, Betty opened one eye to look at her vase of flowers and then closed her eyes. Within seconds, she seemed to be deeply asleep. We crept out of the room and down the stairs.

As we were leaving, I asked Linda if she'd ever heard of the name Kingsfield.

'Funny you should ask that. Someone else mentioned Kingsfield a few days ago. I can't remember who, but I can tell you it's a farm – well, a smallholding really.'

'Do you know who lives there?'

Linda shook her head. 'No one. Not any more. It's been derelict for at least five years.'

Nineteen

Linda Parks stared thoughtfully into space for a moment. 'I've just remembered who mentioned Kingsfield. It was Jan Thomas, one of the RNs. She used to go out there. She called it the Hammer House of Horrors.'

'What did she mean by that?'

Linda was about to reply when her mobile rang a cheerful tune. 'I'll be about five minutes,' she said in answer to her call.

'I've got to go,' she said. 'What a morning! Have you heard about Grace Pattingham disappearing? Even pensioners aren't safe these days. She used to work at our centre.' I opened my mouth to ask more, but Linda was rushing to her car. Annie was also about to go, but she stopped and said, 'Try the Parkside Health Centre receptionist. She loves a good gossip.'

As I walked away, I thought maybe I was on to something, but what? If Kingsfield had been a connection between those who were attacked, it was now derelict, so how could that help? Was I wasting my time?

The Co-op funeral parlour's office was empty now of both staff and clients. The door was open, so I hovered there, and within a minute or so, a grey-haired rotund man with glasses on a chain around his neck came towards me, hand outstretched. 'I'm the director, Gordon Croft – how may I help you?'

'I'm not a client. My name's Kate – I'm a private investigator.'

'You live with old Hubert, don't you?' He was smiling, his round face giving the impression of an elderly baby, all pink and smooth.

'I'm his lodger,' I said primly.

'What can I do for you, Kate?'

'I'm trying to help in the search for Grace Pattingham, and one or two names have cropped up. I thought you might be just the man to help me.'

'I'll give it a try,' he said cheerfully. 'You sit down and I'll fix us a coffee.'

The coffee didn't take long to 'fix' from the Thermos flask.

'Now then,' he said as he handed me the coffee. 'Test my memory. I can remember every funeral of the last ten years. That's how long I've been here. It is a funeral, is it?'

'Yes. But I only have a first name – Freda.'

He slipped his glasses on and peered at me. 'We've had a few Freda's die over the last ten years.'

'This one had three children and she'd had a long illness.'

'Grown-up children, I presume?' he asked. I nodded.

Gordon looked thoughtful. Then he smiled. 'You're in luck. I do remember the funeral. There were only five mourners, which is unusual when there are adult children. They chose our most expensive coffin and she was buried with the family photos.'

'What did she die of?' I asked.

'My memory is not that good.' He laughed. 'You hang on here and I'll check on our computer.'

When he came back a few minutes later, he said cheerily, 'Armstrong, that was the name. The daughter, Barbara, was the eldest by a good few years, then came Michael, then the youngest, Anthony.'

'Cause of death?'

'The death certificate gave cause of death as pneumonia and arteriosclerosis. She'd had a stroke twenty years before. From the notes I made at the time, it seems the three of them had nursed her all that time. One of the lads carried on working while the other two looked after their mother.'

'What about the other mourners?'

He thought for a moment. 'There were only two. A health visitor and a district nurse.'

'You wouldn't by any chance know their names?'

'Well yes. One was Grace Pattingham ... Coincidence that, isn't it? She was the health visitor for the elderly in the district, and Jan Thomas – I know her fairly well.'

Gordon sipped thoughtfully at his coffee. I took a single careful sip – it was bitter and undrinkable. I placed the cup on the tray in front of me and waited.

'I'm trying to remember,' he said, 'what became of Barbara and Michael. Barbara, it seems, was a trained nurse. She left Kingsfield and no one has seen her since; and Michael closed down his shoe-repair shop about a year ago. He said people didn't walk much any more, and bought new shoes instead of getting them repaired.'

'Where is he now?'

'No idea. I haven't seen him.'

'What about Anthony?'

'He's around. Works at Harry's Place. They call him Tone – I think it makes him feel younger.'

'I've seen him in there,' I said casually. 'I don't suppose you know where he lives?'

Gordon shook his head. 'I'm not the font of all knowledge,' he said, 'but I did hear he didn't see his brother any more.'

I thanked him profusely and left. At long last, I seemed to be getting somewhere. All roads, it seemed, led to Kingsfield. And the one person who might be able to give me the connection between the rape victims, and now Grace, was Alvira.

I rang Megan to tell her I was on my way. 'I thought you'd deserted us,' she said, her voice full of gentle reproach.

'I need to speak to Alvira. How is she?'

'Very quiet. I think she wants to go home. You won't upset her, will you?'

'I'll try not to, Megan, but it is important. You have heard a woman has been abducted from outside the station?'

'Yes. The local paper said she was missing. You think she's been abducted, do you?'

'I do. And it may be the same man who raped Alvira.'

Megan breathed deeply and muttered, 'Oh dear. I know you're only doing your job. I'll see you later. Alvira has taken Katy for a walk, but she won't be long.'

As I drove up to the house in Farley Wood, Alvira was wheeling Katy into the house. Katy was having a screaming fit, so I sat in the car and waited for ten minutes until I heard the wails subsiding.

When I knocked on the door, it was Alvira who answered it. Megan had obviously forewarned her, and was upstairs with Katy. We sat down in the kitchen and Alvira busied herself making tea with her back to me. 'I've heard about that other poor woman,' she said. 'They haven't found her yet, have they?'

'Not yet,' I said, 'but the more days that pass, the more likely she'll be found dead.'

Alvira eventually finished making a pot of tea and arranged biscuits on a plate. 'I've been thinking,' she said quietly. 'I ought to report it. I have to think about other women. I'm being selfish.'

'No, you're just scared and grieving.'

She picked up a biscuit and stared at it. 'Ginger nuts were my husband's favourite biscuit,' she said. 'I never did like them, but I'll have one now.'

I wasn't sure quite what the significance of that comment was, but she began nibbling the biscuit.

'I want to talk to you about ... Kingsfield,' I said. The half biscuit in her hand fell in her plate noisily. 'How do you know about Kingsfield?'

'Trust me,' I said. 'I'm sure there is a connection between Kingsfield and your attacker.'

'What sort of connection?'

'I don't know until you tell me.'

There was a long pause before she said, 'I suppose it doesn't matter now. Times have changed. I'll tell you about Kingsfield.' She sighed sadly. 'I was eighteen and working in a grocery shop. The owner died and the shop was eventually sold. Longborough was much smaller then and there were very few jobs. A living-in job came up at Kingsfield Farm, mother's-help-cum-skivvy really, but I had a nice room, food, and the pay was the same as at the shop. It meant I could help my mother out. Anyway, Freda Armstrong had a three-year-old called Barbara. Lovely little tot. But Freda wanted a boy. So I looked after her while Freda cleaned and cooked. Nowadays you'd say she had an obsessive condition. In those days cleanliness was next to godliness. Anyway, I used to take her husband Norman's packed lunch out to him, especially at harvest time. And we got friendly. I didn't know anything about sex in those days, or sexual frustration, but Norman told me that he and his wife hadn't slept together since Barbara had been born.' She paused to sip her tea. 'Anyway, three years went by and I didn't get pregnant. He said he was "careful" – but he wasn't careful enough. I did get pregnant. I kept it a secret for as long as I could, then I told Norman. He said he wanted to divorce Freda and marry me, but that would mean selling the farm. In the end, he gave me enough money to go away for a few months. I had the baby, a boy, and he was adopted.'

'He's never tried to trace you?'

She shook her head sadly. 'No, but he lives in my imagination. He's having a good life. He's a farmer like his dad. He's got two lovely children and a pretty easy-going wife who loves him.'

'But...' I began.

'I'm happy the way things are,' she said firmly. 'I don't have to worry about him. He's fine.'

'Did your husband know about your son?'

'Yes. He wanted children but I never conceived again.'

'What about the Armstrongs?'

'Well, I heard later there had been other mother's helpers before and after me. I was truthful when I said I didn't know Ivy ... but Barbara had a doll that she called Ivy.'

'What about a Betty?'

'No, I don't remember a Betty.'

'What about Freda's sons?'

'I left before they were born. He obviously managed to share her bed after I'd gone.'

'Have you seen Barbara since?'

'No ... I wish I had. I did hear she became a nurse, but I never actually saw her. She was a very intelligent child. Reading well at the age of four.'

'And Norman?'

'I heard he'd died. Twenty years ago now. I

know we did wrong, but he was a lovely man. You never forget your first love, do you?'

I agreed. 'How did he die?' I asked.

'An accident. It was in the paper. Barbara was about twenty-two then. She was driving a tractor and she reversed over him. I heard it made her ill and Freda suffered a stroke almost immediately afterwards.'

'So it fell to the boys to look after her?'

'Yes, but Barbara did most of the nursing.'

'So have you seen the sons since?'

There was a slight pause. 'Yes. I couldn't fail to recognize Michael. Good-looking, quite chatty. He had a little business in Longborough.'

'Doing shoe repairs?'

'Yes, that's right. And engraving and making locks and keys. I took my husband's shoes there. He liked expensive shoes and it was worthwhile having them mended.'

'What about keys? Did you have any keys cut there?'

She looked puzzled. 'I can't remember. I know we lost a key once. I may have, but he only did keys the last few years he was in business. Is it important?'

'It might be,' I said. 'And what about Anthony?'

'I never met him.'

'You're sure?'

'As sure as I can be.'

'Does Michael still live in Longborough?'

'I haven't seen him in years.'

'Nor Barbara?'

'No. I think she went away as soon as her mother died. They couldn't carry on living in that farm – it was falling down.'

Megan coughed before coming into the kitchen. 'I don't want to disturb you but I'm dying for a cup of tea. I'm hoarse from singing lullabies.'

We sat for a while chatting, and Alvira came with me to the front door. 'Why all this interest in Kingsfield?' she asked, frowning. 'What good does it do to rake over the past? It was so long ago. It was another life.'

'It's said the past shapes the present, and if raking through old happenings helps to find Grace, and catch a rapist, then it will be worth it. Thanks for telling me.'

She smiled sadly and hugged me. As she drew back, she said, 'There is one more thing. It's not important, I'm sure ... but once Norman and I were caught ... making love ... by Barbara. She was only a child, but afterwards she behaved oddly towards me ... gave me little knowing looks.' She broke off. 'I don't know why I told you that, but I do wonder if it affected her in any way.'

As I left, I realized that the Armstrongs may have been more than a family under stress, and there was a connection with Kingsfield for Ivy, Alvira and Betty – but what about Alice? And where was poor Grace? And why her?

Twenty

David rang that evening. 'There is some good news,' he said. 'Do you want the good news or the bad news first?'

'Just tell me,' I said. I wasn't in the best of moods, as I'd had words with Hubert and now he was sulking in his office.

'First,' he said, 'Tina Burrows has been charged with the murder of her daughter. She's admitted it. It seems *she* was the religious fanatic, and the fact that her daughter had lost her virginity sent her over the edge.'

I wasn't surprised. Having met Tina, the poor woman was obviously deeply disturbed.

'Will they say it was diminished responsibility?' I asked.

'I should think so,' said David. 'The police surgeon is recommending a psychiatric hospital, as she's likely to try to harm herself.'

'Poor woman,' I muttered.

'Yeah. Anyway, next bit of news. A lucky charm from Grace Pattingham's bracelet has been found about three miles out of town on a grass verge. She may have managed to throw it from a moving car, or it may have come off in a struggle. Either way, Kate, it seems we're now looking for a body.'

'And the good news?'

'The good news is, young Lianne has walked into a police station in Scotland. It seems her pick-up was pre-planned, whereas her pregnancy wasn't. She was so scared of her parents' reaction, she decided to disappear. Conscience got the better of her and she's reported in, but she doesn't want to return to Longborough.'

'So where does that lead us with Grace?' I asked.

'Waterworth is in real trouble with those above. The finding of the charm managed to swing it for him. There's a team scouring that area at the moment. Give it a day or two and then he'll arrange a reconstruction at the station. It might just jog a memory or two.'

I told him about Kingsfield, and that Alice was the odd one out as concerned the Kingsfield connection. 'I'll check it out when I've got time,' he said.

'Nothing of Grace on the CCTV cameras?' I asked as an afterthought.

'A blurred image of Grace leaving the station, that's all. Whoever positioned the cameras was a moron.'

David told me he'd 'catch up with me' sometime, and I was left feeling a little deflated. I was sure he wasn't taking much notice of my interest in the Armstrongs. He hadn't asked any questions, and I supposed that was because he was preoccupied with organizing the reconstruction.

Hubert decided to put in an appearance about an hour later. His sulking was obviously past, because he managed a conciliatory smile. When I told him about Tone and Michael, he said, 'I'll find out their addresses for you.'

I glanced at his expression. He looked shifty. 'You're in touch with Harry, aren't you?' I said. 'You sly old bugger.'

'Not so much of the old, Kate. And yes, he's been in touch and he'll be back at work in a couple of days. He's still upset, but he says Alice would have wanted him to get on with his life – so he's going to try.'

'I don't want to arouse any suspicions in the Armstrongs – I might be wrong.'

'You often are,' he said with a grin, 'but this time you could be right.'

'Do you really thing so?'

'No. But it's worth a try.'

Again I felt a bit deflated, but I wasn't deterred. While Hubert cooked supper, I rang Frank Pattingham. His answering 'hello' was barely a whisper.

'How are you coping?' I asked.

'I'm not. The police are doing a recon-struction tomorrow. Maybe someone will remember something.'

Tentatively I asked, 'Grace's charm brace-let?'

'What about it?'

'Have the police told you they found one of the charms?'

'Yes. They didn't seem to think that it was a very good sign. They've told me I must prepare myself for bad news.'

'Grace may have been trying to give the police a clue, or starting a trail. You know, like Hansel and Gretel.'

There was a pause before he answered. 'The police showed it to me – the charm – so that I could identify it.'

'What was it?'

'A cat.'

'I think, Frank, that's a hopeful sign. Perhaps Grace was giving us a clue.'

'What does it mean?' he asked.

'I don't know, but I'll keep in touch.'

He murmured his thanks and I hastily put down the phone. I didn't want to raise his hopes when Grace might well be dead. After all, why keep her alive to be a witness? But if it was the rapist who had abducted her, he hadn't killed his other rape victims, so why kill Grace? But then, why wasn't she freed once he'd raped her? Had she died of hypothermia in woods perhaps miles from Longborough?'

'Supper's ready,' called Hubert.

Hubert, well over his sulk, was in chatty mood. 'What's next,' he asked, 'in your investigating calendar?'

I knew exactly what I was going to do next, but I didn't want Hubert to know. He would think it was a waste of time. So I muttered something about visiting Michael and Tone when he found out their addresses for me.

We sat down to watch TV later, and I kept yawning, hoping it would have an effect on Hubert, who already had Jasper in a hypnotic trance, induced by Hubert's stroking. After a while of my yawning, even Jasper began to yawn, and it wasn't long before Hubert commented on how tired he felt, and that he was going to bed. He handed Jasper over to me, and I lied and said there was a film I wanted to watch. Hubert, a tad suspiciously, said, 'I didn't know you were interested in kung fu films.'

'I'm not so tired now,' I said.

'Could have fooled me,' he replied somewhat sourly.

I waited for an hour and then crept out of the house with Jasper under my arm. I drove out of the car park with one eye on Hubert's curtains, but I didn't see them twitch and I soon began to relax. I knew I was being fool-hardy, but fear is hard to sustain. After a while, as in war zones, you have to get back to normal life with a *bugger the bombs* mentality.

I was about two miles from Longborough when it began to rain and rain and rain. There was little traffic and Jasper lay doggo on the back seat while I drove on hoping to find Kingsfield Farm. I drove through dark villages and hamlets and eventually found the village of Carterhatch, which I knew to be the village nearest to Kingsfield. More by luck than judgement, I found a single-track road deeply pitted and overgrown, at the end of which I was sure I would find the farm.

A barred gate at the end of the track meant I could go no further without getting out of the car. Jasper was most reluctant and howl-ed in disbelief, but I slipped on his lead and ignored his protests and we stepped out into the torrential rain and the black night.

By the light of my torch I slipped the rope from the gate and saw ahead of us the dark shape of an old farmhouse. The sound of the rain and the slurp of my shoes in the mud, plus Jasper's occasional high-pitched whine, were aural reminders of this being a fool-hardy exercise. I'd wanted to make sure the farmhouse really was derelict. Certainly, at first glance, the rotted window frames and hanging guttering that spewed rain on to the porch were a good indication that it wasn't habitable. As I got closer, I could see that dark curtains, as torn and as dilapidated as the outside, had been pulled closed.

Jasper needed coaxing and pulling towards the porch. Once there and away from the water pouring from the gutter, he began pawing at the front door. It had been painted a dark brown once, but it was rotten top and bottom, though someone had secured it with an iron bar and a padlock. I shone my torch through the letterbox. I couldn't see much, but I could smell damp and decay. What I could see were uncarpeted stairs with the banister half hanging off and some mail strewn on the floor.

Jasper began to whine loudly. I guessed he wanted to go inside. He protested but we went round to the back door. That too was sealed with a padlock. I managed a glimpse of the kitchen, or at least part of it, through a gap in the curtain. Just a kitchen table covered with a plastic cloth and a shiny black teapot in the middle of the table. Jasper tugged at the bottom of my jeans and it was obvious there was nothing to be gained from staying any longer, except pneumonia.

Back in the car with the heating on, I

rubbed Jasper down with an old car rug and wished someone was there to do the same for me. We steamed gently on the way home and crept in quietly for fear of waking Hubert.

As I slipped beneath the duvet that night, I thought how futile my visit had been – what had I expected to find anyway? Had I hoped to find evidence that someone was living there? A mad rapist keeping Grace prisoner? At least I'd seen the place for myself, and there seemed no doubt that it was indeed just an empty shell.

In the morning at breakfast Hubert was in interrogation mode. 'Where did you get to last night?' he asked.

'Jasper needed to go out,' I said.

'In the pouring rain?'

'Needs must,' I said.

'There's no need to lie, Kate. I heard the car.' He paused. 'And you left muddy foot-prints everywhere.'

'That's an exaggeration,' I said. 'If you must know, I went to Kingsfield.'

'Why?'

'That's a good question. I just wanted to make sure it really was derelict.'

'And was it?'

I nodded. 'Yes. Padlocked front and back. As quiet as the grave.'

We both looked at each other. 'You don't

think,' I said, 'that Grace has been buried there?'

Hubert looked undecided. 'Leave it. The police will check it out.'

Hubert went down to his office about half an hour later and returned within minutes to give me the addresses of Michael and Tone. He handed over the slip of paper somewhat reluctantly. 'How are you going to manage this?' he asked. 'If one of them is the guilty party, you could be in danger, or more to the point, you could cock up the whole investigation.'

'I'll be careful,' I said. 'Anyway, I have a cunning plan.'

Hubert sighed loudly. 'Your planning skills are similar to your mother's ability to up sticks and go whenever the fancy takes her.'

'Well there you are then. She survives. She gets through.'

'Just try to be a bit professional.'

I gave Hubert what I hoped was a withering glance. Not that he noticed. It was becoming obvious to me that we were holding each other back. Maybe I should be more like my mother – have curling tongs, will travel.

Once Hubert had gone, I glanced at the addresses he'd given. I was surprised to find that Michael Armstrong lived in Carterhatch. Was he responsible for the padlocks

218

on the door? It seemed likely. He didn't know me and I wondered if I could pass as a prospective buyer for a rundown property. It was worth a try. How to dress for the occasion was a problem. Should I look like a rich-bitch property developer or a land lover who wants nothing more than to wade through mud in green wellies and keep pigs and chickens?

The reconstruction was taking place at the same time Grace had disappeared – around eight p.m. I had all day to seek out the Armstrong brothers.

I decided to visit Michael as a country lover; my wardrobe didn't boast anything that shouted money, and dressing down came far more naturally to me.

Wearing jeans, a tired-looking navy jumper, a padded gilet and green wellies, I scraped my hair back from my naked face and stared at myself in the mirror. Yes, I could imagine myself mucking out pigs.

I found 'The Cottage' in Carterhatch easily enough. Carterhatch hardly qualified as a village. There was one shop, selling so called 'antiques', a pub and about ten houses. The Cottage had a thatched roof and tiny windows, but a large front and rear garden. An old dark-blue Astra was parked outside, and I noted the number mentally.

The red front door looked freshly painted

and the lion's-head doorknocker was a handsome gold colour. I knocked several times and was about to explore the back of the house when the front door finally opened.

Michael Armstrong bore little likeness to his brother. Of medium height, and slim with a slight stoop and floppy dark hair, he appeared more the academic type than a cobbler or ex-cobbler. He had tired hazel eyes and a network of lines around his mouth and eyes. World-weary would have described his face. 'What do you want?' he asked sharply.

'I was making enquiries about properties in the area...' He didn't let me finish.

'This house isn't for sale.' He was about to shut the door on me, so I said quickly, 'Not here – Kingsfield.'

He studied my face carefully. 'Who are you? How do you know about Kingsfield?'

A particle of truth often helps, so I said, 'Harry from Harry's Place in Longborough told me about you owning a smallholding. It's a dream of mine to move to the country and keep chickens and pigs.'

A half smile crossed his face. 'You a single woman?' he asked.

'Yes. Does that matter?'

'Of course it matters. To run a smallhold-ing properly you need a man about the place or unlimited money.'

'I've got money,' I said. 'I'm willing to pay a fair price.'

'Who do you intend to pay that to then?'

'Well, to you of course,' I replied.

At that moment a telephone rang and he turned with a distracted look. 'You'd better come in,' he said. As he closed the door behind me, I saw the telephone on a small hall table, and as it rang, it became obvious he had no intention of answering it.

Twenty-One

The telephone rang and rang. We both stared at it as if mesmerized. A little flicker of unease began to grow. Not only was I behind a closed door, but he stood in front of the door, effectively barring my way out. 'Are you going to answer it?' I asked. He shook his head. 'Bound to be a wrong number. I don't get many calls.' Once the ringing stopped, there was a moment of silence when he looked slightly confused, as if wondering what I was doing in his cottage.

'Come through to the kitchen,' he said.

I followed him through the gloomy interior to the kitchen. Although the kitchen only had a small window on to the back garden, the walls had been painted a sunny yellow. There was a breakfast bar with one stool, but hopefully I wouldn't be there long enough to need to sit down. 'Fancy a cup of tea?' he asked. He pointed to a black shiny teapot, a match for the one at Kingsfield. I declined, even though my mouth was dry. I stood by the open kitchen door, aware that he was staring at me with an expression, not exactly of lust, but the sort of look that falls between sexual interest and general curiosity. It struck me then that not many women crossed his threshold. I may have looked like a dishevelled farmhand, but perhaps that look turned him on, or he was so desperate he didn't care.

'If you don't want to sell Kingsfield to me, I'd best be off,' I said.

'We haven't discussed it yet, have we?' He moved closer to me. So close I could see he had dandruff on his black cardigan. My interest in his discarded scales caused me to notice the cardigan was hand-knitted. Unusual, I thought, especially as it looked fairly new. 'That's a nice cardigan,' I commented.

'I knit in the evenings,' he said. 'Do you knit?'

'No.' I didn't elaborate. I wanted out.

'Now then, about Kingsfield,' he said. 'You want to buy it?'

'Yes. But you don't seem to want to sell it.'

'It's not mine to sell.'

'Oh. I thought...'

'You thought wrong. My sister inherited the farm and she chooses not to sell it.' That was something I hadn't thought of, having assumed the Armstrong children would have equal shares.

'If I could meet her,' I said. 'Perhaps I

could persuade her.'

'I doubt it. She's adamant. She wants it to rot away. The thought of anyone living there appals her.'

'Why's that?'

'My sister has been ill for many years.'

'I'm sorry about that.' Then I added casually, 'Does she live in Longborough?'

'No. But I can contact her.'

'Could I phone her?'

'No. She doesn't talk to strangers.'

'Not much I can do, then, but thank you for your time and I'll be on my way.'

He gave a slight shrug, as if he felt he'd missed an opportunity. 'You wouldn't be interested in seeing some of my knitting, would you?' he asked. 'I'm looking for sales outlets and word of mouth always helps.'

I wanted to look at his knitting slightly less than to have a dose of Lassa fever, but I also wanted to keep him onside, so I agreed.

He showed me into the tiny front room and went upstairs. I hurried over to the mantelpiece to look more closely at the family photos arranged there. There were only three. Each one featured Christmas. A white-haired old lady sat in bed surrounded by her children – Anthony, Michael and Barbara. The silver Christmas tree – about ten inches – sat on the bedside table. Anthony and Michael looked a little younger but otherwise hadn't changed. Barbara was as tall as Anthony and wore a long skirt with black socks. Her dark hair was cropped short and her features were strong and masculine. In fact, she looked like a man in drag.

I didn't hear footsteps behind, but suddenly Michael was behind me holding a huge armful of his hand knits. 'We had a hard time looking after the old girl,' he said quietly in my ear. 'But now it doesn't seem so bad. We were a team in those days.'

'Why did you split up?' I asked.

'Barbara became ill again after mother died. She didn't have a purpose any more. We'd run the farm down when mother needed more help, and once the animals had gone, we lost interest in maintaining the house. We all had enough money, I sold my business and we sold off tractors and bits of land to neighbouring farms. Anthony went to work in Longborough and I moved here.'

'You seem young to retire,' I said.

He ignored that comment and placed his pile of jumpers and cardigans on the two-seater sofa. 'Now, you sit down,' he said, 'and choose one as a present.'

'I couldn't possibly do that. I'll pay you for one.'

'No you won't. Just choose one – it's yours.'

I was no expert on hand knits. An auntie

had once knitted me a school cardigan in bottle green when our school colours were navy. After two washes it felt as rough as a man's beard, so I was somewhat skeptical until I began to feel them. These garments were soft and delicate, knitted beautifully, with decorative extras like pearl buttons and silk linings. I was more than impressed. 'Go on,' he said. 'Choose one.'

'I'll buy one,' I said.

'Which one?' he asked.

I held up a cardigan in softest green with tiny pearl buttons. 'Hold it to your face,' he said. I held it against me. 'It's your colour,' he said. 'It suits you. Alice was going to buy that one.' I dropped the cardigan as if it were on fire. 'You mean dead Alice?'

'Yes, poor Alice. She'd bought one or two of my designs. She died before that one was delivered.'

My mouth had now completely dried. I struggled to find my voice. 'Do you have a list of customers?' I croaked.

'Of course. It's not a long list. Mostly old customers of mine. And a few people that Anthony knows from the café.'

'Anthony delivers them, does he?'

'Yes. He's in Longborough. I haven't got any customers around here yet. He's got the cheerful-chappie approach. I'm the more serious one. I'm not a good salesman.'

'You've sold me one,' I said. 'And I'd be really grateful if I could have a look at your list of customers.'

'Why?'

'Just curiosity really.'

He gave me a puzzled look but from a bookshelf handed me a notebook. Inside were dates, prices, and colours, types of wool and names and addresses. There were about twenty or so names – among them Ivy, Alvira, Alice and Betty. The very last entry was Grace Pattingham.

Michael meanwhile was rooting around in a cupboard. Eventually he found what he was looking for – a plastic bag. He folded the cardigan carefully and handed it to me wrapped in the plastic bag. I hastily got out my purse. 'I won't accept money,' he said softly. 'But if you'll let me take you out to dinner wearing it, that would be payment enough.'

At that moment, I would have promised him life-long commitment just to get out of the place. I hurriedly took his phone number, saying I would ring him the next day and, clutching the cardigan, I rushed towards my car.

I waved cheerily as I drove away, then parked my car round a corner and phoned David. There was no reply, so I left a message saying I had important information and would he get back to me ASAP.

Then I sat for a while thinking about cardigans and connections. And Anthony – 'Tone'. My plan was to see him next, but he knew what I did for a living, so maybe I'd try a different tactic or maybe not. Perhaps I really did want a smallholding in the country, and as the younger brother, maybe he had more influence over his sister than Michael did.

I drove back to Longborough and decided to forewarn Tone that I wanted a private chat with him and could I visit him after work that evening.

Harry's Place was even busier than usual, but I managed a seat and shared a table with a very large man who was actually sharing half my seat as well. He was twice as big as the average person and his portions were trebled. He'd ordered three baguettes, a large bag of crisps and a jumbo-size milk-shake. He sat, jowls trembling, as he stared at the food as intently as any voyeur at a peephole. My appetite diminished, and when Sal took my order for a round of toast, no butter, and a black coffee, she didn't seem surprised. 'Swings and roundabouts,' she muttered.

'Did you know,' I asked cheerfully, 'that Tone's brother is a great knitter, and designs the most fabulous cardies and jumpers.'

'Yeah, they are great. I've got a couple, and

so cheap too. He's a bit of a genius.'

'What about Tone, has he got any hidden talents?'

She looked towards the counter, where he was filling orders and making the customers laugh. 'He has – he's a great mimic. He can take anyone off. He only has to hear a voice once and he can sound just like them.'

'Must come in handy,' I said.

'It cheers people up,' she said. 'Everyone needs a laugh.'

The big man beside me had demolished all his food and was slurping his way through the milkshake whilst I still nibbled daintily on my toast. As he got up to leave, he did have a comment to make: 'Black coffee's not good for you, love.' I watched his rolling buttocks move to the door. They were almost independently alive. He had to turn sideways to get out of the door, but he gave me a cheery grin and pointed a warning finger at me.

It was Tone who came to offer me a refill for my coffee. 'I'll have some milk this time – the big man told me black coffee was bad for me.'

'He was a sixteen-stone weakling before he started coming in here,' laughed Tone, giving the Formica table a thorough wipe over.

'I wondered if we could have a private chat after you finish work.' Then I added casually,

'Perhaps at your place?'

'What about?'

'Just a business idea. I'm not making any money as a PI.'

As more customers walked in, he said, 'Yeah, OK. Six thirty. Number eighty-six Temple Drive.'

So easy, I thought. Pity, though, that it wasn't after the reconstruction, then David could have been involved. I didn't particularly want to be alone with him, but I wanted to follow things up as soon as possible.

Back at Humberstone's, I tried David again. He still wasn't responding. Hubert was between funerals and seemed busy and preoccupied, so I merely told him I'd seen Michael and that he didn't own Kingsfield and that he wasn't very forthcoming about his sister, who did.

'I heard a rumour today,' said Hubert, 'that Barbara Armstrong was taken away from Kingsfield by men in white coats. That was five years ago, and no one's seen her since.'

'Maybe she's the catalyst,' I muttered.

'Does it matter what the cause is?' asked Hubert. 'Whatever is wrong with her isn't contagious.'

'Maybe it's catching,' I suggested.

'Like irritation?'

'Don't mock. Some families just have the unhappy burden of being...' I paused.

'Totally bonkers,' said Hubert, giving me a patronizing pat on the arm.

'I was going to say – disturbed.'

'Just tell David what you know and stay away from them. I've got a feeling they are bad news.'

I had the same feeling, and before I went to see a potential rapist, I needed a bit more background. I rang the health centre and asked to speak to district nurse Jan Thomas. She was in a meeting that would end in half an hour.

At Parkside Health Centre, the reception-ist was off sick, but I managed to find Jan having tea alone in the staff room. She was in her thirties, short and round, with a cheery smile, a soft voice and an infectious laugh. When I mentioned the Armstrongs, her cheeriness faded a little. 'Before I say anything, I have to consider confidentiality. If my manager agrees, I'll tell you about them.'

'Tell your manager,' I said, 'that the information you give may help find Grace – dead or alive.'

I expected Jan to be surprised by that, but she wasn't.

She came back within minutes to say her manager had agreed to my being informed of the general nursing set-up at the farm, and of the nursing care given by the family to Mrs Armstrong. Other private details, family history-wise, were not to be disclosed.

Jan had first visited Kingsfield as a new district nurse. 'That was nearly seven years ago. I think they sent me there to test my initiative. Afterwards I found out that no one went more than twice. I managed four or five visits.'

'So you got to know them quite well?'

Jan laughed. 'I wouldn't say that. I found out after my first visit that the others called it "The Hammer House of Horrors". I dreaded going. The atmosphere was so oppressive.'

'Tell me about your very first visit,' I said.

Twenty-Two

Jan settled herself back in the chair. 'Mrs Armstrong had a stroke in her fifties. She had youth on her side then, and she managed to get round on a Zimmer frame, but she had trouble speaking. Not that she had any trouble letting her wishes be known.'

'How do you mean?' I asked.

Jan smiled ruefully. 'Her word was law. She wanted no changes made to the farm while she was alive. No mod cons at all, and after her death, she wanted the place to rot and the land to be sold.'

'So conditions there were poor?'

'Poor! That's an understatement. Conditions there were abysmal. There was no hot-water supply. A coal fire, so that only the back room where Freda was nursed had heating. The old range was never used, and Barbara used to cook on a little Belling cooker. One lavatory that often didn't flush and wallpaper that hung off the walls due to damp. Freda only survived because of Barbara's obsessive care.'

Jan fumbled in her shoulder bag and eventually found a packet of mints and offered me one. She crunched on it thoughtfully. 'By the time I made my first assessment visit, most of the farmland and the animals had been sold off and Barbara, Michael and Anthony concentrated all their efforts on looking after Mum. That day, Barbara had complained of backache and I said I'd blanket bath her mother. What a performance! The water took forever to heat, then Barbara stood over me like a hawk. The water wasn't hot enough; the towels had to be warm. Each towel was colour-coded with little ribbons so that I didn't use the wrong one. She had four flannels, also colour-coded. Her hands and feet had to be soaked and massaged with cream. There were four different types of cream. By this time I was a dithering idiot. At one point I put her back cream on her feet and the old lady kicked me.'

'What about the sons?' I asked.

'They lurked outside the door, ready to lift her out of bed.'

'Did she have a wheelchair?'

'No. She sat in an ordinary armchair with a commode beside her.'

'How long had she lived like that?'

'At least ten years. It was like a mini ward. Barbara slept in a single bed beside her. She ventured outside of that room occasionally to do a bit of dusting. Michael ran his business and Anthony helped Barbara. It seems he did most of the shopping and cooking.'

'It sounds claustrophobic.'

Jan laughed. 'It was. I thought it was very unhealthy. Barbara acted like some 1950s matron. She wrote a daily report on her mother and a night report. If a doctor had visited, he'd have been shown fluid balance charts, blood pressure charts. She even tested her mother's urine and cholesterol levels. Barbara ran a hospital containing one highly demanding patient.'

'So, she didn't see a doctor?'

'No. Mrs Armstrong made her wishes clear – she didn't need or wish to see a doctor. To be honest, Barbara kept her going all those years. Gave her physiotherapy, kept her mind stimulated.'

'But she sacrificed her life.'

'Oh yes. And of course, when the old girl died, it was Barbara who fell apart. She stopped eating, stopped washing and spent most of her time in bed. It was Michael who sought help for her when she started hearing voices and wandering about the house at night trying to find her mother.'

'So Barbara was taken off to hospital?'

'Yes. And the boys moved out – bought places of their own and got on with their lives.'

'Is Barbara still in hospital?'

'No idea. No one's seen her since a month or so after the funeral.'

'Did Grace see the family?'

'She visited every three months or so. She tried her best to encourage them to put their mother in respite care but they wouldn't hear of it. She was worried about them all, but particularly Barbara.'

'Did you have any worries about Anthony?' I asked.

'Not in particular, but I know Grace found him odd.'

'In what way?'

'When his mother was alive, he was a real loner, but now he works at Harry's Place he seems fine, although...'

'Although what?'

Jan frowned slightly. 'I once asked him about Barbara and he nearly bit my head off. He said she was fine and there was no need to ask. Sometimes I wonder if she's even alive.'

'She'd be buried beside her mother, surely, if she'd died?'

Jan didn't seem convinced.

'Which hospital would she have been taken to?' I asked.

'The nearest psychiatric hospital is sixty miles away – Danetree Park...' She paused for a moment. 'Tell you what, I'll give them a ring and find out if she's still a patient.'

Jan disappeared for several minutes and then returned looking a tad anxious. 'What's the matter?' I asked.

'Nothing really,' she murmured thoughtfully. 'Barbara was discharged six months ago. It seems she was to go to a halfway house with resident psychiatric staff, but she failed to turn up.'

'How ill is she?'

'The charge nurse said she had Florence Nightingale delusions, his own diagnosis, and wanted to nurse everyone. At night she took to wandering around with a torch and waking the other patients. She'd offer them water and question them about their general health. For a while the staff had to lock her in at night. I think she was a real pain. The new homely environment, it was hoped, would change her behaviour.'

'Has she been classed as missing?'

'I don't think so. She wasn't considered a danger to herself or anyone else. She was a free agent.'

'Thanks for finding that out,' I said.

'Will it help?'

'Yes. I think so.'

I was about to leave when Jan said, 'Don't get the wrong impression about the Armstrongs. I admired their fortitude and the superb care they gave to their mother. But underneath all that, it was a battle for control. Barbara is definitely a control freak, but tried to make it appear that her mother was calling the shots. As for Michael and Anthony, they were totally dominated by both women. It's amazing they've turned out OK.'

'Yes, isn't it?' I muttered.

At six thirty I was in Temple Drive knocking on the door of Tone's bungalow. I could hear movement inside but it took ages for the door to be opened. When it was, I was convinced I'd come to the wrong house. For the door was opened by a woman in a wheelchair wearing a pink tracksuit. She was in her fifties, with greying hair and a round face. Her distorted hands showed evidence of rheumatoid arthritis. 'I'm sorry, I think I must have the wrong address,' I murmured in embarrassment.

'It's Anthony you want, isn't it? He'll only be a few minutes. Please come in and wait. He said you'd be popping round. I'm Ruth and you must be Kate?'

I followed her into the spacious bungalow through a wide hall and into an open-plan living room. She manouvered the chair into the kitchen area and asked if I wanted tea. I declined, partly because I didn't want to see her struggle.

'Isn't this bungalow wonderful?' she said happily. 'Anthony did all the work himself. I'm so lucky to have met him.'

A hollow pit welled in my stomach. My unease began to grow as she told me how they had met in a local supermarket a year ago, when he'd offered to help her with her shopping. She'd been living on her own since her husband had walked out on her and she was finding it hard to cope.

'Then along came Anthony – my knight in shining armour. In three months he'd altered this bungalow to cope with the wheelchair, and we've been together ever since.'

'And he doesn't miss the single life?'

She smiled. 'No. He says he's never been happier just staying in every evening and looking after me.' She paused. 'I do as much as I can, of course – I do most of the cooking.'

An awkward silence followed. Ruth glanced at the wall clock. 'He's later than usual.' There was a slight trace of anxiety in her voice, but after a moment she said, 'I expect it's Harry who's delayed him. I don't know if you've heard, but Harry is thinking of selling up and moving on ... since Alice.'

'I hadn't heard. Has he got a buyer?'

'Not yet. He only mentioned it on the phone yesterday. But if he does sell up, I know Anthony would be interested in taking over. If...'

'If what?'

'His sister was left a farm in their mother's will, but she's refusing to sell...'

'Are you telling Kate all our family secrets?' Anthony stood in the doorway smiling. Neither of us had heard him.

'You gave me a shock,' said Ruth. 'I didn't hear you come in.'

He moved towards her. 'You're a deaf old bat,' he said, kissing her lightly on the lips.

'I was just telling Kate about Harry wanting to sell up.'

'You know the score, love,' he said gently. 'Barbara won't hear of anyone else living at Kingsfield.'

I already felt in the way and was eager to leave, so I said, 'I should really be off. It was Kingsfield I wanted to talk to you about.'

'What about it?'

'My business is ... well ... not exactly thriving, and I thought Kingsfield ... if the price was right ... might be what I'm looking for.'

'For what?' he asked sharply.

'Bed and Breakfast, keep a few chickens, plant some fruit trees – you know, the rural idyll.'

He laughed dryly. 'I've heard of it. Living in the country is about mud and cold and isolation. Believe me – I know. I lived there for years. Hated every bloody minute of it.'

'Well, it was just an idea. Anyway, it's your sister I should be speaking to. Could you tell me her address?'

'I've got no idea,' he said sharply. 'I've got no idea where she is, but I know she wouldn't sell the farm – ever.'

'Oh well,' I said as I stood up to go. 'I shall just have to keep on looking.'

'Stay and have supper with us,' said Ruth.

'It's kind of you, but Hubert's expecting me back and he's cooking. I'd best not be late.'

Anthony stood behind Ruth's wheelchair at the front door as they waved me goodbye. Somehow it made a sad little scenario. Her knight in shining armour was more likely to be the man in the black balaclava.

Twenty-Three

The reconstruction of Grace Pattingham's abduction meant that the station had to be taped off to allow the stand-in to pause alone outside the station. Uniformed police almost outnumbered the brave onlookers who'd come out on a cold and windy night. I stood beside Hubert with my collar up, wishing my ears weren't so cold and wondering how long it would be before something happened. I scanned the police for a sighting of David. When I did catch a glimpse of him, it was inside the station itself by the ticket office, so I had no hope of speaking to him then.

Some onlookers grew bored with waiting, so Hubert and I moved nearer to the police tape. 'Hello,' said a voice beside me. It was Frank Pattingham. He looked gaunt, his eyes sunken, his face grey in the street light. 'Shouldn't you be with the police?' I said.

'I've had enough of the police and their questions,' he answered. 'This is what they do when there is no hope left.'

242

'It could jog someone's memory,' I said. 'It's happened in the past.'

'We'll see,' he said, unconvinced.

Silence fell on the small crowd as we heard the train coming in. As the passengers emerged into the ticket hall, they paused, seeing their exit was taped off and police with notebooks were everywhere. Last to emerge was Grace's lookalike. She was about five foot six, with greying hair cut in a classy bob. She wore a black skirt and jacket and a red polo-neck sweater. The skirt ended two inches above her knees and she wore black leather boots.

Frank swayed at my side. I grabbed his elbow and Hubert moved to his other side. 'I can't believe it,' he said croakily. 'She's the image of Grace.'

I couldn't believe it either. 'When was that photo of Grace taken that you keep in your wallet?' I asked.

He looked slightly mystified. I knew the camera could lie but this was a mega lie.

'Just before she retired,' he said. 'It was a lovely shot of the kitten.'

The lookalike before us looked at least ten years younger. She was smart, fit-looking and glamorous. In the dark, she might have been mistaken for a woman in her prime, not an OAP. All my theories about the rapist only targeting elderly women faded. Or this could have been a random unplanned pick-up by a man who thought black boots and a glimpse of knee meant only one thing.

Poor old Frank either needed glasses or he'd been married so long he didn't notice how his wife looked any more.

The sound of 'Quiet Please!' echoed from a megaphone. It was Waterworth. His second 'Quiet Please!' was on cue and with slightly more emphasis. 'Our stand-in for Mrs Grace Pattingham will now repeat her walk from the platform through to the booking office. There she will be seen using a mobile phone. Outside, there will be a moment when she appears distracted, as if someone is calling her name. She will also throw a mobile phone on to the grass verge.'

I guessed that Waterworth was reading from a prepared statement, as he hadn't repeated himself. He cleared his throat and said, 'If anyone remembers...' Suddenly a shout went up, 'I remember!' A raised hand was in the air. A buzz of renewed interest circulated. A uniformed officer was already approaching an elderly man propping up his bicycle at the side of the station. The PC listened for a few minutes then approached David. The elderly man was whisked to another part of the station, out of sight, and a few moments later 'Grace' appeared again, this time pausing at the entrance.

Frank gave a huge sigh when it was all over. 'That chap seemed to know something. When will they tell me?'

'I don't know,' I said. 'Depends what he saw or thinks he saw.'

Gradually the crowd dispersed, leaving two or three people making statements and Frank looking lost and frightened. For some reason his daughter wasn't with him. So Hubert offered to drive him home. 'The police drove me here,' said Frank, 'but I'd appreciate a lift.'

As they drove away, I guessed Hubert would be home late. Hubert was a good listener and Frank was a man who needed to talk.

I went in search of David then, but could not find him or the man with the bicycle. I was bursting with information and I tried him by mobile phone but his answer machine was still switched on. Dispirited, I wandered down Station Road wondering what to do next. Betty's light was on and I dithered outside, debating about disturbing her. I knocked on the door and her very tall nephew promptly answered it. 'She's much better,' he said. 'She's downstairs today.'

Betty looked pale and was wrapped in crocheted blankets, but she was smiling and seemed quite chipper. 'Hello, love. Nice to see you. Thank you for the flowers – lovely they were.'

Her nephew went off to the kitchen to make tea, giving me a chance to ask her about any hand-knitted cardigans or jumpers she may have bought.

'No, dear,' she said, frowning. 'I don't buy many clothes, and if I do, I get them off catalogues.' She paused. 'Hang on ... I did buy something hand-knitted ... a bedjacket. Why do you ask?'

'It could be important. Where did you get it from?'

'A friend ordered it for me. A bloke brought it round.'

'Had you seen him before?'

'No. He was in his forties, dark hair, sort of ordinary. Nice enough.'

'Did you ask him in?'

'No.'

Her nephew came in with a tray holding mugs and a black shiny teapot. 'I 'ope you gave that a good wash,' she said to him sternly. 'I never use that one and it's been sitting on an open shelf for ages gathering dust.'

I stared at the teapot and felt a little shiver of excitement. The teapot on the table at Kingsfield was supposed to have been sitting there for five years – undisturbed. Someone had dusted it recently. There was no doubt in my mind that it was Barbara and she was living there.

'You all right love?' asked Betty. 'You look like a mouse just ran up yer trouser leg.'

'I'm fine. I just remembered something. The man who delivered the bedjacket – could he possibly have been your attacker?'

Betty shrugged. 'I dunno. The way I feel at the moment, it could be Prince Charles that raped me. I've already told you what I noticed about him, but since me heart attack, I've got a bit forgetful. I'm trying to remember when I got that bedjacket … Six months ago – I just don't know.' Her voice had begun to fade and I could see she was tiring. Her silent nephew looked anxiously on, so I made my farewells and left.

Hubert did return late that night. I was dozing on the sofa having failed to rouse David on three more occasions. I'd stopped leaving messages and had begun to think he really didn't want to speak to me. Then, just as Hubert walked in, my mobile phone rang. Hubert was pouring himself a brandy and, when I saw it was David, I launched into my pent-up account of hand knits, teapots with no dust, and Barbara, who I suddenly decided could well be dead and buried alongside Grace.

'Hang on, Kate,' he said softly, as though talking to a mad woman. 'Just take it slowly. Firstly, your chief suspect has alibis for the

247

nights of the rape.'

'His girlfriend Ruth?'

'Yes.'

'She adores him. She's bound to lie for him.'

'Well, she's lied very convincingly. I've seen her this evening. Seen them both.'

'How did you get on to them anyway?'

'It was Betty – she's sharp and she mentioned Kingsfield. So, we've been out there but the place is falling down and our health and safety man said—'

'You have a health and safety man on the job?' I was incredulous.

'Think about it,' he said. 'If the stairs collapsed on one of our PCs and he or she broke their neck – can you imagine the compensation?'

'Cops risk their lives every day.'

'They do, but that place is an obvious hazard. It's a risk not worth taking, since there's no one there. We have done an outside search.'

'There could be bodies inside.'

'Yes,' he said slowly, 'and we're doing our best to find the owner, Barbara Armstrong, so that we can go in legitimately. Her brothers say they don't know where she is.'

'They're lying.'

'Well, if they are, we'll find out.'

He was so calm and his tone so condescending that I found myself swearing under my breath. But then I reminded myself that health and safety were the buzz words in all public services today. Nurses and carers very rarely lifted patients any more. A mechanical hoist was either accepted or the patient wasn't moved. Fear of litigation had affected so many professions that it wasn't surprising a derelict building was seen as an unacceptable hazard.

'There is one more development,' he said. 'An old man was riding by on his bike when he saw Grace getting into a car...'

'Did he get the number?'

'No. But he recognized the make – an old Vauxhall Astra, either dark-green or dark-blue, he's not sure which.'

'And the driver?' I asked impatiently.

'I was coming to that. The driver stayed in the car and opened the door. Grace got in, and according to our witness, they seemed 'friendly'.

'How friendly?' I asked. 'Was it tongue down the throat or a peck on the cheek?'

'More of a hug, but seconds later as they drove away, Grace threw her mobile phone out of the car.'

'And I suppose the bad news is they didn't get a glimpse of the driver's face.'

'Got it in one. Just that he had short hair and a turned-up collar.'

'Why did she throw her mobile phone away?' I murmured.

'We're checking phone records on that one,' said David, 'And of course trying to trace the car. My bet is it'll be found burnt out somewhere, perhaps miles from here.'

'I suppose it's a breakthrough,' I said, not sounding too convinced.

'There's just one more thing we've found out. Grace has very poor vision. She had to give up driving and she's on medication for high blood pressure.'

On that rather gloomy note, we said goodbye. And I sat staring into space. What was the significance of Grace having poor sight? Did she approach the car not quite recognizing the driver but recognizing his voice? Once in the car, was the hug more of a grapple, resulting in her jettisoning her mobile phone?'

'Kate – fancy a snack?' Hubert's voice jolted me back to reality.

'Great,' I said.

'Nothing like the offer of food to bring you back to earth.'

Hubert was obviously feeling left out, so I told him exactly what David had told me. Hubert, of course, had a slightly different take on events. 'We've all assumed that little 'ol Grace was some elderly lady nearly ready for a shawl and a footstool. According to her husband, she suddenly started wearing fashionable clothes about a year ago and wanting to be more adventurous. Even mentioned doing a bungee jump...'

'What are you trying to say?' I asked, confused.

'I'm saying that Grace had become more of a "goer", and when that happens there can be another man involved.'

'Surely not,' I said, shocked. 'You really think that – just as her husband is on his way to collect her – her lover passes by and she jumps in a car with him?'

'If the car had been a smart sports job would you be so sure she'd been abducted?'

Hubert, looking self-satisfied, busied himself by putting bread in the toaster. 'Another thing,' said Hubert, watching the toaster. 'Even Frank couldn't tell the police what his wife had been wearing that day – he was long married and had ceased to notice what his wife wore. He loves her dearly but he did take her for granted.'

'I can't believe it,' I said. I felt almost as rattled as if he'd just told me my mother had entered a nunnery.

As the toaster pinged, Hubert removed the toast and began buttering. 'You didn't know Grace at all,' he said smugly. 'Once she left health visiting, she didn't have to be a stereotypical respectable health worker any more.

Perhaps it was a spur of the moment decision. Her husband wasn't there to meet her at the station. She was peeved and then when her lover turns up she decides, on impulse, to go away with him.'

I knew when Hubert started using long words like 'stereotypical' I was on to a loser. I didn't want to be convinced that Grace was no better than my fly-by-night mother – she was older than my mother was anyway.

We agreed to disagree, and when Hubert had gone to bed, I sat with Jasper on my lap and mumbled away to him. If the police began to think like Hubert, and Grace was simply a runaway adult, would they also downgrade their investigation into the rapes? Would Barbara simply be yet another missing adult? More to the point, was Anthony or Michael going to remain free to rape again?

Twenty-Four

The next morning I rang Alvira to ask her if she'd ever bought a hand knit.

'I haven't,' she said. 'But my husband bought me one as a present for my birthday. Is it important?'

'It might be. Do you know who delivered it?'

'No. It was a complete surprise. It's an exquisite cardigan. It's blue with an embroidered butterfly at the front, and the buttons are unique, with a little blue stone in each one. I only wear it on special occasions. My husband had very good taste.'

I thanked her and gave Michael Armstrong – cobbler and key smith – some more consideration. I thought back to his home and my previous experience of people who indulged in hand knitting as opposed to machine knitting. Wool and knitting needles are portable. There is usually some evidence of a knitter in the house – balls of wool, knitting patterns, needles, even the odd loose threads on the carpet. I hadn't shaken hands with him, but his hands were large and dry-looking. No doubt the palms were calloused from years of cobbling. There was no way he had knitted such delicate items. In the long years of her mother's illness, Barbara would have been the one to sit knitting in the long winter evenings. But was she still knitting? Was Michael selling off old stock?

I'd given some thought to Hubert's theory that Grace had a lover, but I was no more convinced. I was far more convinced that Anthony was the rapist and that he left home at night and made his way to his well-targeted victims. Getting Ruth to admit that might be impossible, but I had to try.

Before going to the bungalow, I checked that Tone was behind the counter at Harry's Place. I'd decided to take Jasper with me, hoping that Ruth liked dogs. Jasper can have a relaxing effect, and if Ruth was relaxed, she might just give something away.

She looked tired and worried when she opened the door, but she smiled and invited me in. She insisted on making me tea. The taps had been specially adapted and the electric kettle had a grip fitted. All in all, she managed really well, but it made me very conscious of how difficult such mundane tasks were for her. And just how much she relied on Anthony.

When we were settled with our tea and she

had admired Jasper's impeccable behaviour, which he managed on occasions, she said, 'We've had a visit from the police. They wanted to know if Anthony ever went out at night.'

'What did they think he'd done?'

'Something serious. They didn't say. I don't think they wanted to upset me, because I'm disabled. But I'm not a child. And I can put two and two together.'

'What do you think they are investigating?' I asked.

'Burglary. It's stupid. He's the most honest man I've ever met. I told them that. We go to bed early – about ten. He has to help me wash and undress because I can't move my arms above my head. Then he helps me to get into bed. And in the night, if I need the toilet, he helps me out of bed. I can walk a few steps though – but I do sway a bit, so it helps if he's behind me.'

'Do you have a double bed?'

She eyed me with slight suspicion, but then smiled and said good-naturedly, 'I know what you're thinking. We sleep in single beds, just in case he accidentally knocks against me. I'm on steroids and I bruise very easily. But we do make love, not often, admittedly, because Anthony is a very gentle person and he does worry about me.'

Again I had that nasty feeling in the pit of

my stomach, knowing that her cosy life was about to be unravelled. 'Have you ever woken up and found him not there?' I asked.

This time her look was wary, but I sensed she'd resigned herself to answering questions that she felt could prove Anthony's total reliability.

'I take a sleeping tablet with a cup of cocoa and a couple of biscuits,' she said. 'The steroids make me hungry. And I usually sleep until about three or four in the morning. Anthony is always there for me. And usually sound asleep.'

There was no point in saying that he had plenty of time in the hours before three a.m. to leave their home. Rapists do get away with their crimes, and I had a feeling that Anthony was going to do just that.

As I left, she gave me a wan smile and said sadly, 'I really hope this will be the last of it.'

'So do I.'

'I hope whoever is paying you,' she said, 'will realize that Anthony is not a suspect for anything. He's a good man.'

I smiled and said nothing.

The next day and the day after, there appeared to be a no-news situation. I felt I'd reached an impasse. What else could I do? I had a feeling the police now shared the belief that Grace had been picked up by her lover.

For lack of anything else to do, and because nobody required my paid services, I decided, as the day was bright and crisp, to go out to Kingsfield again. This time I might manage somehow to get inside the house and have a proper look around.

As before, I left my car at the barred gate and began walking towards the gloomy farmhouse. I'd only walked a couple of paces when I became aware of movement in a clump of bushes. I walked on, but the back of my neck prickled. Someone was watching me. I had a strong inclination just to run back to the car. I had a torch, a mobile phone and my car keys in my jacket pocket. Not much in the way of weapons, but I was wearing leather boots with a sturdy heel, so I thought, when in doubt, I could rake down his shins. My unease grew when I heard more cracking from the bushes, like footsteps on branches.

'I know you're there,' I shouted. 'You'd better come out.'

No one did, so I moved towards the clump of bushes. 'Oh, all right,' said a small voice, and from the bushes emerged a small boy and a bike. I guessed he was about ten years old. He had fair hair and flat pugnacious features. 'I wasn't doing nothing,' he said.

I said, 'That's all right then. Why aren't you at school?'

'Got the pox,' he said. Then he added helpfully, 'Chickenpox.'

'I've had that,' I said.

'What you doing round 'ere?' he asked.

'I wasn't doing nothing,' I answered.

He smiled at that. 'That's two of us doing nothing then.'

'No one lives in the farmhouse, do they?' I queried.

'Not in the day.'

'What do you mean?'

'I think it's haunted, and there's rats in there as big as that.' He expanded his hands to about twelve inches.

'Have you seen them?'

'Nah, but I've heard them.'

'So you've been inside?'

'Yeah. Once or twice. Only with a mate. It's too scary to go in on yer own.'

'Why is it scary?'

He looked at me as if I was stupid. 'The noises from the rats. It's worse at night.'

'So you've been inside at night?'

'Yeah. Once, with a mate. Only downstairs. The floorboards are a bit dodgy and upstairs is where the rats are.'

'Would you take me inside?'

'What the bloody 'ell for?' he asked, which was a sensible question.

'Do you want the truth?'

'You're not one of them perverts, are you?'

'No, I'm a private detective.'

He laughed. 'And I'm in MI5.'

'Straight up,' I said, showing him my business card. He stared at it for a moment and then asked, 'Do you do murders and stuff like that?'

'Sometimes I investigate murders.'

'What about stolen cars?'

'No, unless it's important.'

'What about a reward?'

'For what?'

'Finding a stolen car.'

'That could be worth twenty quid.'

'Make it twenty-five and I'll show you. You can follow me in yer car if you like.'

'OK. What's your name?'

'Jack.'

'Lead the way, Jack.'

I followed him on his bike for about half a mile down a track parallel to the farm. At the end of the track, at the side of an empty field, was a ramshackle shed. Before I'd stopped the car, Jack was kicking open the door. I peered inside – there was plenty of light, because half the roof was missing. Inside, amongst rotting straw and rusted farm implements, was a dark-blue Astra.

'Well, Jack,' I said. 'That's worth twenty-five pounds. Thanks. How did you know it was stolen?'

'Just a guess. It wasn't here a week ago.

And it's taxed. Must be nicked, mustn't it?'

'I think you're right,' I said, handing him the twenty-five pounds. He looked at it, counted it, folded it carefully and pushed it down his right sock. 'Have you ever seen anyone hanging around or going inside?' I asked.

'Nah. I'm at school ... when I'm not off sick.'

'And you've never seen anyone inside?'

He gave me an old-fashioned look. 'I'm not stupid. As me mum says, farmers round 'ere 'ave shotguns. There was that bloke who shot the burglar. I read it in the papers. I wouldn't go near the place if I thought there was a mad farmer living there.'

'Fair enough,' I said. 'How about us getting in the farmhouse?'

'What's the time?'

'One thirty.'

'I'll 'ave to ring me mum.' He took his mobile phone from the pocket of his jeans and jabbed out the number. I could hear his mother shouting that he was late, but he seemed used to it and simply said, 'I'm on me way, Mum.'

'Tell you what,' he said, 'if you come back tonight, I'll get my mate and we'll get you into Kingsfield. It'll cost you though.'

'Why can't we do it in the light?'

'My mate's at school and then he 'as to do

his 'omework and 'ave his tea. Can't do it before eight, and I 'ave to be in by nine.'

'What will you tell your mum?'

'I tell 'er I'm round Danny's place. She never checks as long as I keep ringing 'er.'

'Right then,' I said. 'I'll see you by the gate at eight.'

'Don't be late. Cost you another thirty, cos Danny will want his share.'

I watched the little entrepreneur cycle quickly away. Meanwhile, his mother was deceptively consoled about his whereabouts by his use of a mobile phone. Jack was the type of child who'd ring his mother or answer his mobile phone if he was stuck on a roof or halfway up a tree. But I supposed ignorance was bliss in those circumstances.

I'd decided I could use the same tactic with Hubert. I knew he wouldn't approve of me being in the rural hinterland after dark, and I didn't want him to come with me as he might scare off the boys. I'd think of something in the meantime.

I rang David then, and, to my surprise, he took my call. Before I'd had a chance to say anything, he said, 'I need a drink. Will you meet me in the Crown in half an hour?'

'I've got some info,' I said.

'So have I,' he answered.

Twenty-Five

The Crown was busy around the bar, but the lounge itself was quiet and we found a place near the window where thin sunshine and a mock coal fire made the place seem warmer. Or at least more warm than David's mood. 'I've had it up to here,' he said, thin-lipped and whacking himself under the jaw.

'Waterworth?' I queried.

'Yeah, stupid old git. He thinks Grace has run off with a lover and he's only just beginning to take an interest in the whereabouts of Barbara. It seems the hospital she was in has suddenly realized she only had two months' medication with her. They now fear for her safety.' He paused to drink half his pint of beer in one go. 'And more to the point, Waterworth has downgraded the operation to one DC, allocated solely to the rapes. He spends all his time in front of a computer checking known sex offenders.'

'What reason does he give for the downgrade?'

'He says, since only Betty has come forward, and that didn't offer us any forensic evidence, we must wait till he strikes again. The public should be vigilant and aware that, unless rapes are reported, rapists won't be caught.'

'Try telling that to a ninety-year-old,' I murmured.

By the time he'd nearly finished his pint of beer, David seemed a bit more relaxed, and when I told him I'd found what was probably Grace's lover's car, fully taxed and abandoned in a shed near Kingsfield, he cheered up considerably. I gave him the number and thought he'd be impatient to get away but he wasn't. 'I'm going to have another pint,' he said. Then he added in the same breath, 'Marry me, Kate.' I thought I'd misheard, so although my mouth dropped open, I kept quiet. After a brief pause, I said, 'I should go and get that pint. I think you need it.'

'I need you more,' he said.

I watched his retreating back. He was far more stressed than I'd realized. I knew he'd be embarrassed when he realized what he'd said, but I have to admit I was a bit gratified. After all, it was my first proposal. I'd lived with a cop, but even the *word* 'marry' would have choked him.

He came back with his pint and a glass of white wine for me. 'Have you thought about it?' he asked.

'Was I supposed to? I thought it was spoken in grateful thanks for me finding the car.'

'You can be very irritating,' he said with the slightest of smiles.

'There you are then,' I said. 'Not only are you not in love with me, you find me irritating. At this stage you should think I'm perfect.'

'You are for me.'

'This is very sudden,' I said, choosing my words carefully. 'Are you sure stress isn't affecting your judgement?'

'No. If anything, I'm seeing things more clearly.'

He took my hand and patted it. 'Give it some thought,' he said, as if his proposal was on a par with buying a second car.

'I'll do that,' I said. 'In the meantime, what about Barbara and Grace?'

David smiled at me benignly. 'Leave it to me. We'll get a trace on the number plate. That should give us something to work on, and we'll use the media to help us find Barbara. This time, we'll use a more recent photo.'

'If there is one.'

'Good point. Since she hasn't been seen for six months, her appearance may well have changed.'

Now that David had finished his second pint, he seemed keen to get back to work. He insisted on walking me back to Humberstone's and kissing me at my front door. It was OK. 'You'll have to do better than that if you're serious.'

'I am,' he said, giving me another peck on the lips. 'You just wait and see. I'm a fast learner.'

It was only when I found Hubert in the kitchen making sandwiches that I realized David had not offered to feed me. The chances of a positive response to his offer plummeted from a six out of ten to a four out of ten.

I debated for a while if I should tell Hubert about my unromantic proposal, but decided against it. It would mean questions and debate, and there were other more important things going on. So I told him about finding the car.

'That's a breakthrough,' he said. 'How did you manage that then?'

'Cunning and ingenuity, of course.'

'Oh yeah. Who helped you?'

'If you must know, it was a kid called Jack. Ten years old and off school with chicken-pox.'

'Did he nick it? Or was it his older brother?'

'Neither, he's a nice kid. And he's bright,

because he noticed it had been taxed, so he figured out it wasn't just old and abandoned.'

'Have you told David?'

'Yes. He knows. I saw him at the pub. He's checking it out.'

Two hours later, David rang me. 'Thought you'd like to know,' he said. 'We've checked out the car. It's registered to ... Barbara Armstrong. We'll be picking it up in the morning and giving it to the forensics boys to check over.'

'Great.'

'Is it OK if I pick you up tonight and take you out for a meal?' he asked as my heart sank.

'I can only make it later. About ten?'

'What's so important?' he asked.

I paused. Already I had to state my whereabouts.

'Just a friend I promised to visit at eight.'

'OK. Don't be late. I'll be starving.'

As I put down the phone, I caught a glimpse of my prospective future. It didn't include eating out late in expensive restaurants. It meant having to be at home with a meal on the go to suit the vagaries of CID investigations. My life would no longer be my own. I had a feeling he would also expect me to iron his shirts. In return for what? Regular sex? I could get that elsewhere if I put my mind to it. Housekeeping money? I managed. Even if the agency failed, I could get a job. Companionship? I wouldn't get much of that, because he'd always be working. A joint mortgage? A possibility, I thought, although paying rent suited me. So, in the final analysis, it came down to his pension, which was a long way off. Sorry, David, I thought, no can do.

I arrived early at Kingsfield, having told Hubert I was driving out to see Megan and Alvira. I'd be back in an hour or so, and I reasoned he need never know I was out in the country after dark.

It was a cold, clear night with a visible half moon. I sat in the car with the engine running and the heating on and sucked mints. I glanced at my watch just before eight, then at five past. By ten past I was growing worried. At twenty past I thought of abandoning the whole event, which was probably one of my more duff ideas anyway.

As I sucked yet another mint, I nearly choked as someone banged on the boot of my car. I swung round to see Jack's face, nose even more flattened against my back window. An older boy was by his side, wearing one of those slinky helmets that motorbike riders wear. 'Couldn't 'elp being late,' said Jack by way of apology. 'This is Danny.'

They left their bikes propped against my car and we tramped towards the black and eyeless farmhouse. The half moon provided some light, so we didn't need our torches yet.

The boys led me round the back of the house and pointed by torchlight to a small boarded-up window about five feet or so above the ground. It looked as if the brick-work underneath was newer than the sur-rounding bricks, as if once there had been a door there.

'It's the bog,' explained Jack.

'That window is tiny,' I said. 'You'll get stuck.'

'Nah,' he said. 'I've done it before. Once I take me jacket off, I'm skin and bone.'

He was right. He stripped down to his vest and Danny gave him a bunk up, and just as I was wondering how he'd manage to remove the boarding, he punched the edge so that the piece of board opened like a door. I was impressed – and even more impressed when he began to slither through sideways. His shoulders were narrow, but at hip level I wondered if he'd become stuck. 'Give us a push then,' he gasped. We both pushed hard on his legs, and I could hear his jeans snag-ging and some less than childish swearing as he finally got through the window. I heard no crash on the other side but I obviously looked worried. 'It's all right,' said Danny. 'The bog's got one of them old-fashioned cisterns. He's grabbed the pipe. He's like a monkey. He's landed on his feet.'

Danny began walking round to the front of the house. I followed and still wondered how the hell we were going to gain entry with the chain and padlock on the door. As we approached the door, I heard a bolt being drawn back and then a key was put through the letterbox. Danny picked up the key and turned it in the padlock. The chain fell clinking on to the concrete porch. 'You wouldn't think people could be that stupid,' he said.

Once inside, he handed Jack his clothes. Blue-lipped and shivering, Jack quickly got dressed. 'Well done, mate,' said Danny, giving his friend a slap on the back.

'Someone's been in 'ere after us,' said Jack. 'That bolt on the bottom of the door wasn't bolted before, and the key was under the mat.'

'You did well to find the key,' I said. 'Especially in the dark.'

'Yeah well. Me mum always puts a key under the front door mat. And they put theirs on the inside. Daft, innit?'

I nodded in agreement. Now I had guilty feelings about Jack. He seemed to have real prowess as a burglar, and he knew how to extract money. Was I encouraging him down the proverbial slippery slope towards a life where the words 'basic' and 'enhanced' related only to prison regimes?

Both Jack and Danny had their own torches, so we explored downstairs. Jack, buoyed up by his exploit, did a running commentary. 'Cor, I'm telling you, this place is worse than mine, and me mum says my room's a pigsty. And don't it stink? 'It's 'orrible.'

He stopped by a rolled-up piece of carpet, looked down and then up at the ceiling listening. 'Can't 'ear any rats, can you?'

Danny and I both said no in unison. 'Good,' said Jack. 'Cos I'm scared of rats.' Then he added, 'I'm not coming in the kitchen.'

'Why not?'

'There's a rocking chair in there just like the one in that film, *Psycho*.'

Downstairs, there was a small hallway with the stairs straight ahead. The bannister was coming away from the wall and by torchlight the dodgy state of the stairs themselves was obvious. There were two main rooms. The larger of the two had no furniture at all. The other room boasted two straight-backed dining chairs and a faded floral three-piece suite, very fashionable once – about 1930. Dust was everywhere. I ran my finger along the mantelpiece and over the only ornament, a plain, once white vase. My finger was black.

'I don't like it here,' said Jack. 'It's 'orrible and creepy. I reckon there's ghosts.'

'I thought you didn't believe in ghosts,' said Danny.

'I do now! And I believe in rats.' Jack's face looked pale by torchlight. He was beginning to lose his nerve, which seemed healthy to me. My nerve too was slowly slipping away.

'I bet you haven't seen a rat ever,' said Danny, trying to act the tough guy.

'I've seen the film *The Rats*,' said Jack defensively, 'and I've seen a documentary.'

'Well, get you,' said Danny. 'Ain't you the world's leading expert?'

'Shut your face,' responded Jack.

'I'll go and look in the kitchen,' I said. 'You two stay here and stop arguing.'

In the kitchen, the black teapot was still there as I remembered it. I shone my torch directly on it and again wiped a finger over it. My finger was clean. Someone had dusted it recently. I turned on the tap. The water was still on. I doubted if the electric supply was still on, but I flicked the light switch just to make sure. Then I realized there was no bulb beneath the dusty plastic shade.

When I got back to the boys, Jack was just finishing a call on his mobile. 'I gotta go. Me mum wants to go out, so I've got to look after me little sister. 'ave you got the money?'

I handed over the money. What else could I do? I'd hoped that Danny would stay, but they were both keen to go, and I wondered if Jack's call to go home hadn't been a ploy to get away.

'You staying then?' asked Jack.

'I'll just have a bit more of a look round.'

'Mind the rats,' he said, grinning.

They may have only been young boys, but they were company, and three torches were far more comforting than one.

I stood looking up the stairs and listening. I couldn't hear any rats but if there was a body up there, and by now I was convinced there was, I wasn't sure I could face the sight of rats feeding off a corpse. Or even corpses. If Barbara had been killed by Anthony or Michael, or both, soon after she left hospital, there would be no flesh for the rats to eat. But if Grace's body was up there, the rats would still be eating her. It was just as well that the boys had gone. I wouldn't have let them see anything, but I could have impressed them with my bravery.

I began the ascent of the staircase, guessing that the part of the stairs nearest the wall would be strongest. Each stair creaked under my weight, but the first three held. Only another nine to go, I told myself.

I began to hear noises I hadn't heard

before. A slight rustling, a sound like water trickling along a pipe. The creaking of the fourth stair seemed to echo. My right leg began to tremble. I couldn't do it on my own. I needed help. I fumbled in my pocket for my mobile phone. I leant against the wall and was about to punch out Hubert's number when the stair began to crack. I moved up swiftly to the next stair, but in my panic and with both hands occupied, I dropped my phone.

I shone my torch downwards, but couldn't see my mobile. I tried to convince myself that I wasn't meant to have help. It wasn't in the stars. 'Right then, just go for it!' I said aloud as I rushed up the remaining stairs. I found myself on bare floorboards in a narrow corridor with four doors leading off. It reminded me of some ghastly game show. Choose the right door and win the prize. Except that this was for real. And above me something scrabbled in the attic.

Twenty-Six

I carefully opened the first door just a fraction, then kicked it wide open. I'd seen it done in films and, with my torch held like a gun, I shone the beam into the room before going further in. Nothing moved, because the room was empty. The carpet had been rolled up and stacked in a corner. There was no furniture or bed. The next two doors I opened revealed equally empty dusty rooms. On the landing was a wooden chair, and I looked up to see pull-down aluminium steps leading to a large loft door.

By now I was beginning to feel a little braver. I stood on the chair and realized that, with such a low ceiling, I could easily pull the steps down. In reality it wasn't that easy, but I managed it and began the ascent. Three steps from the top, I gave the loft door a tentative push. It began to open, but something was coming towards me. By the time I saw that it was a shoe, I was catapulted to the floor. All my fears disappeared in a vast black hole as my head hit the floorboards.

* ★ ★

I was dimly aware that I was lying on a hard surface and being moved. I couldn't open my eyes, because I felt far too sleepy. It felt as if I was floating upwards. If this was dying, it felt OK. And if I was just dreaming, it felt OK too. I couldn't think properly, but I wasn't worried. It was like being very drunk and just wanting to sleep.

When I woke, everything was dim but with a reddish hue. From the ceiling hung a black tasselled shade, the red light bulb beneath hardly registering any light, but at least I wasn't yet an angel. I looked sideways to see that there was a clock on the wall. At first I couldn't focus on the hands, and then I thought I'd lost the ability to tell the time. The big hand is straight up, I told myself, and the little hand is on the eleven. I blinked and saw two clocks. But now I knew it was eleven o'clock. Not that knowing the time helped me in any way. I closed my eyes, aware that I was in bed.

A quiet voice beside me said, 'Go back to sleep. You're in hospital.' I felt a stinging sensation in my arm and thought, *Good, I'm getting morphine or pethidine – so no pain.* Then came more oblivion.

It was a whisper that woke me. 'Wake up,'

said a female voice. 'Open your eyes.'

'Where am I? What's happened?'

'She's gone for now, but she'll be back,' she whispered. 'I'm Grace.'

I tried to turn my head to the voice but couldn't.

'Don't worry,' she said. 'She's got you in a homemade neck brace. It's two stone hot-water bottles covered in towels. She kicked you down the ladder – do you remember?'

Don't worry! I thought. 'Have I broken my neck?' I asked.

'No, she wants you to think that.'

'Why?'

'She's mad. Who are you?'

'I'm Kate. I'm a private investigator.'

'She'll be back any minute, Kate. Just keep quiet. I can't move, she's put my arm in a sling, my right leg is in a splint and my other leg is tied to the bedpost.'

My thoughts were as jumbled as a bag of jigsaw pieces. 'What happened to you?' I asked.

'She stopped at the station. I thought she wanted to chat. She opened the car door and yanked me in.'

'Who did?' I asked, although it would have been patently obvious to me if I'd had an unmedicated brain.

'Barbara Armstrong.'

'Why's she doing this?'

'She's deranged. She's paranoid. She thinks the police have been after her for years.'

I struggled to get a grip on what was happening. If I moved my head restraints, would I end up crippled? My head felt fuzzy and I couldn't decide what I should do.

'She's up to something,' whispered Grace fearfully. 'She's been doping me up, so I pretend to be asleep most of the time. She's phoned her brother. They've found your car. I think they're planning to get us out of here.'

'Where to?'

'I don't know. She mentioned the council wanted to demolish this place, because it's unsafe. I think it's panicked her. And you turning up.'

'I've got my mobile...' I broke off as I remembered I'd dropped it. I looked down at myself. I was stark naked. I too started to panic when I realized I couldn't move my feet. 'I can't move my feet,' I said plaintively.

'Don't worry,' said Grace. 'It's the bedclothes – she pulls them really tight. Try again.'

I wiggled my right big toe, then the other one. I wasn't paralysed, and knowing that gave me the confidence to move the dead weight of the stone bottle from the right side of my neck.

'We'll be out of here in no time,' I promised.

My optimism lasted as long as a potato crisp lasts on the tongue. Just long enough for me to sit up and sway. The sound of the trapdoor opening and the sight of Barbara's furious face thrust me back into despondency. She was standing over me in seconds, pushing me back on the bed. 'Silly girl!' she said. She was at least five feet ten and her dark hair had been cut in a short back and sides. The dark-blue uniform with a frilly white cap, black stockings and lace-up shoes made her look ridiculous. I would have laughed normally, or at least suppressed a smile, but she was terrifying. Her lips were thin and tight and her dark eyes shone with maniacal zeal. 'Lie down,' she ordered. 'They'll be after us soon. We'll have to find you a new hospital.'

She turned her back on me to attend to something on a table covered with a white cloth, and as my eyes adjusted to the semi-dark, I looked around the high-beamed room. There were two angled skylights, both covered with black blinds. Grace was lying on a divan bed and I was lying within about four feet of her. By the table was a Z bed. Presumably this was where Barbara slept. To my horror, I also saw a commode in the corner with a bedpan half-covered by a red checked cloth on top of it. My bladder began to squeak in protest. I tried to look up but as I did so Barbara advanced on me with a chart and one of those blood-pressure machines sold in chemist's. She thrust a thermometer under my tongue and the cuff of the machine around my right wrist. It was so bizarre that I wanted to laugh, but if I started, I was sure I'd end up hysterical. Having taken my temperature and blood pressure, she carefully charted them. 'Your blood pressure is up a bit, so it's a salt-free light diet for you.'

'I'm hungry,' I said in a pathetic whinge, hoping it would mean she would have to leave the attic to get me something.

'You can have milk and dry toast,' she said. 'When you've voided.'

It took a second or two for it to click, by which time she was already advancing on the bedpan. 'I don't want to go,' I said. 'And I if I did, I can't get up.' As she bent to get the bedpan, I struggled to sit up. I wasn't going to put up with this. I was getting out. She was, though, the sort who had eyes in the back of her head, like evil radar. As I kicked off the sheets, she put the bedpan down, and just as my feet touched the floor, I saw she had something in her hand and it wasn't the bedpan. It was a syringe. She pushed me back on the bed with one hand. My head hit the stone of the hot-water bottle and I yelled, 'Bugger off!' but she'd grabbed my arm in a vice-like grip above the elbow, and my vein engorged obligingly, so that she injected me effortlessly and then released her grip. The effect was almost immediate. Just time to register it was either Valium or something like it.

'There, that's better,' I heard her say.

I dreamt I was in the cramped room that Anne Frank hid in during the Second World War in Amsterdam. And the Nazi's were coming up the stairs. Somewhere between dreaming and reality, I remembered a visit I'd made to Anne Frank's house. Tourists were everywhere, crowding the exceptionally narrow staircase, and upstairs in that attic room her faded postcards were still on the wall. I'd felt faint with claustrophobia thinking of how many people shared that tiny space – for years – until the fateful day they were found. And still Anne Frank died.

Sunshine woke me. I squinted up at the skylights, which now had the blinds drawn back. Where was I? I was relieved I wasn't still in my nightmare, but I felt so tired. I closed my eyes. I heard voices. One was male. Without stirring and minus some memory, I listened without any real understanding.

'I've done it. They'll stop looking for her now.' I'd heard that voice before.

'Poor Anthony,' said the woman. 'The police won't stop. We have to leave here. They'll come after us when they find out.'

'They won't find out. Not now.'

'They've been after me for years. Even in hospital I wasn't safe. They were watching me. I didn't tell them anything.'

'Look, Babs. We'll be OK if we stick together like we did when Mum was alive.'

'I have to have my patients.'

'We'll find new ones. Really sick ones. You can look after them.'

'I'll need all my equipment.'

'I've got a van. It'll take the beds and—'

I'd drifted off before he was finished. At that moment, I didn't know what they were talking about and I didn't care. Sleep slipped over me as if someone closed the curtains in my brain.

When I woke I was still confused. What the hell was going on? I looked up at the sky-light. It was snowing. My so-called nurse, Barbara, had propped herself on the Z bed. She was fully dressed and snoring. One of those knitting bags with wooden handles was propped by her bed. 'She's asleep,' I heard Grace whisper. I felt sick and dizzy but I managed to sit on the side of the bed and try to get my whirling head straight. I looked around for something to wear but there was nothing, so I was reduced to taking the sheet from the bed and winding it round me. I watched Barbara as closely as a whippet after a rabbit. I moved without taking my eyes from her. At Grace's side, I began undoing her sling and then her splints fashioned from MDF and bandages. It took some undoing. 'I can't see properly,' whispered Grace. I was about to answer her when the trapdoor began to open. I froze on the spot and my knees started to tremble. It was him. I was sure of it.

Twenty-Seven

I raised my foot in an attempt to close the trapdoor, but I was too slow. A wide-eyed little face looked at me in amazement. I put a finger to my lips. Then I whispered, 'Call the police, Jack – now!' I could hear him scrabbling down the steps. Moments later, I heard an engine start up and move off and then nothing.

Barbara woke up. Just for a moment, she too look confused. Luckily I was the centre of her attention, giving Grace a chance to cover up under the bedclothes.

'Get back into bed at once!' she yelled. I did think of trying to take her on, but she looked tough, and if I were injured, Grace would be more vulnerable. I decided instead to try talking to Barbara. 'Why are you doing this?' I asked as I started getting back into bed. She advanced on me and ripped the sheet from around me. 'Now I have to re-make your bed,' she said between gritted teeth. Feeling sure the police were on their way, I was angry enough to forget my previous decision, and with my right fist, I hit her in her solar plexus. It had no effect – she slapped me hard across the face, and as I reeled, she fixed me in an agonizing arm-lock. She forced me on to the bed and began stamping on the floor.

In reply to her stamping, Michael appeared a few seconds later. 'What the hell...?' he began as he took over the armlock. I heard a slight sound that I recognized as a syringe being placed in stainless steel. I struggled frantically but to no avail. 'She's deluded, Michael,' I said in panic. 'The police are on their way. It's too late.'

'It is for you,' he said, as Barbara advanced on me. All I could see was the syringe and its silver needle, and I made one last attempt to throw Michael off. It was as useless as a kitten fighting off a Rottweiler. The needle pierced my skin and within seconds I was no longer in charge of any of my senses.

When I did start coming round, I had one sense left – common sense. I didn't open my eyes immediately. I tried to concentrate on what I could hear and feel. We were moving. The engine sounded loud. And there was someone next to me. For one awful moment, I thought it was a body, a dead body, but then a hand clasped mine. I opened one eye. The only light came from a couple of large torches on the floor. Grace was facing me and we were tied together so that we couldn't move. We were lying on a single mattress in some sort of removal van.

I couldn't see Barbara but Grace could. She signalled to me with her eyes and a slight movement of her head that we were being watched. Her two fingers on my hand told me Barbara was not alone.

An awful feeling of despair and hopelessness came over me. I tried moving my left hand, but that was secured. Both my feet were tied together. I wriggled them continuously, but it made no difference. Grace's nearest was free but I couldn't manage to lean across her to unfasten her other hand without them noticing.

Although feeling defeated, I whispered in Grace's ear that I was sure the police would find us. I wasn't, but it would do no good if we both gave up hope, and she weak and ill. I guessed that Jack hadn't managed to get his message across. Maybe he'd been caught by Michael. Maybe he was even dead. Tears sprang unexpectedly to my eyes, but stopped when I heard them talking.

'You shouldn't have done it,' Barbara said. 'We won't be safe anywhere now.'

'We will,' said Michael. 'In Ireland we'll be safe. They won't find us there. The house is miles from anywhere. We'll live as we did before.'

'I have nightmares,' she said. 'Like I did in hospital. The police catch me and lock me up and you're dead – everybody's dead except me.'

'Come on, Babs. That's not real. We've still got each other. You and me, as we always were in the good old days. We'll grow old together. Nothing will stop us.'

'What about my patients?'

'If they give us any trouble, I'll deal with them.'

I opened my eyes to find Grace's staring back at me in horror. I whispered, 'Say you want to be sick.'

'Help me,' she cried out. 'I feel sick. I'm going to puke.'

As I thought, Barbara immediately reverted to nurse role. She appeared at Grace's side and lifted her head slightly. 'Take some deep breaths. There's a good girl. Just relax.'

Grace gave a bravura performance. She started retching. 'Fetch me a bowl,' Barbara ordered Michael. Michael provided a plastic bowl and Grace obligingly vomited a small amount into it. She was really into the role. I was even more impressed when she started shivering and saying that Barbara was starving her to death.

'What sort of nurse are you?' I demanded, for it seemed to me that we had nothing to lose now. 'She's dying, can't you see that?

You can't even keep healthy people alive, let alone sick ones. You should be ashamed of yourself...' I paused to let my final insult hit home. 'I thought you were a trained nurse. You don't behave like one.'

'That's enough,' said Michael loudly in my ear. I thought he was going to hit me, but Barbara intervened. 'They need a break,' she said. 'We all need a break. Tell him to stop at the next service station.'

I'd already guessed we were on a motor-way, because we hadn't negotiated any corners and the speed of the van rarely dropped. In the meantime, I'd managed to turn my neck far enough around to see that our syringe-happy nurse was opening another ampoule. 'She's overmedicated,' I said. 'You could be struck off for that.' She paused. However ludicrous my warning, it seemed to work. 'This is an anti-emetic,' she said. This woman, I thought wryly, has more drugs than Boots the Chemist does. Had she been stealing them for years, or was someone getting them from the Internet? It was purely academic, but I hoped that if they were out of date they were merely ineffective and not lethal.

'I'll see how she goes,' she said grudgingly, putting down the tools of her distorted profession.

'We're both hungry,' I said. I wasn't at all

hungry, although I couldn't remember when I'd last eaten.

'We'll all eat soon enough,' she muttered.

About fifteen minutes later, we slowed down and stopped. The two of them whispered for a while but I did catch that she wanted the Ladies. I heard the clang of the door shutting and then the key in the lock. I yanked Grace up. In the gloom she looked green. We'd been tied with a mixture of bandages and cord. Working together, we managed to free each other's hands. With our hands free, it was easy enough to extricate our legs. But then what? I picked up the torches, gave one to Grace and said, 'Bang like hell!'

We banged on the door of the lorry and screamed, 'Help!' at the top of our voices. We screamed until we were nearly hoarse and Grace was on her knees, all strength gone. I'd almost despaired, but then we heard the tailgate being unlocked and we sighed with relief – someone had heard us.

Except that that someone was Anthony. He kicked me to the floor, shut the tailgate, and we began driving away at speed.

I sank down to the lorry floor beside Grace, yanked the sheet and blanket from the mattress and put it round us. 'It's going to be all right,' I said, more for my sake than hers. Anthony, meanwhile, sat with his head in his hands muttering to himself. Grace and I clung to each other as the van took a corner violently and brakes screeched. Whoever was driving was driving like a mad man or woman and now it seemed we were in even more peril. I began berating the police for not arriving in time. Even Grace joined in. We crawled over to the mattress and hung on to the sides – and prayed.

After about twenty minutes of hair-raising driving, the van suddenly pulled over and stopped. We were both trembling now, and wondering how much worse it could get. I heard the van door slam. Then came the sound of the back doors being opened and a cold blast hitting us. 'Get out!' shouted Michael. 'Come on, get out.'

Covered just by the one sheet, we moved to the back of the van and looked out. We were on an empty country road in a lay-by. 'You can't leave us here,' I said. 'We'll freeze to death.' He raised his hand to pull me out. I went to take it but, just as I did, Anthony began to make moaning noises and started clutching his chest. Beads of sweat shone on his forehead, and when he looked up, his eyes were pleading and fearful.

'He's having a heart attack,' I said. 'You must ring for an ambulance.' I tried to get nearer to Anthony, but Michael pushed me away. 'Barbara!' he yelled. 'Barbara!'

Twenty-Eight

Barbara's face, when she saw Anthony slumped on the floor, paled. She rushed to his side and cradled him in her arms. 'I'll look after you,' she said as she tenderly stroked his face. 'You'll be fine.'

'He won't, Barbara,' I said. 'He needs an ECG machine, specialist drugs, and an intravenous infusion. If you want him to live, you must call an ambulance – now!'

'He must live,' she snapped. 'He can't die. He's too young. He's my baby.'

Anthony by now seemed semiconscious, and she was rocking him backwards and forwards just as if he was a baby. For a few moments, no one spoke, then Michael said, 'I'm calling an ambulance.'

A strange look passed between him and Barbara. 'Make the call and then run for it,' she said. He took a mobile phone from his pocket and made the call. 'Go, please,' Barbara was saying frantically. 'Don't let them get you.'

Michael knelt down beside his brother and

290

sister and kissed Anthony's clammy forehead and then took Barbara's face in his hands and kissed her full on the lips. I looked away and caught Grace's eye. She raised one eyebrow that spoke volumes.

Barbara gave a cry of anguish as Michael left the van, and I moved nearer to Anthony so that I could feel his pulse. I tried the radial pulse and his jugular pulse. Barbara ignored me as tears slipped slowly down her cheeks. She was holding a dead man.

A few minutes later, the police and ambulance arrived. Grace and I were wrapped in blankets and sat together in the police car, both refusing to go to hospital. Just before the ambulance drove away, we heard Barbara scream.

PC Lisa Hammond, one of our police rescuers, said, 'We've been very worried about you two. Police from three counties have been looking for the van. Are you sure you're not injured?'

'I'm fine,' I said. 'Grace is really weak. Some tomato soup and hot buttered crumpets and I'll be even finer. What about you, Grace?'

She smiled wanly. 'I really fancy bacon and eggs and hot buttered toast.'

Sergeant Brian Davies, the driver, said, 'We're taking you back to Longborough, but if you promise to get checked out at your local hospital, I'll make a little detour to a service station. Mind you, you'll have to eat it in the car – we don't want to frighten the punters.'

There were no hot buttered crumpets, but it didn't matter.

Our 'check-up' at Longborough General was brief. We were both a little dehydrated, but our vital signs were good. Grace's blood pressure was within normal limits, and when we emerged from the examination room, Frank and Hubert were there to meet us. After a tearful reunion, Grace and I hugged and said our goodbyes. The police would interview us in the morning.

Hubert hurried me to his car. I now wore a hospital gown and a red blanket.

'Whatever possessed you? We've been worried sick. If it wasn't for a tip-off from the lad Jack, you might never have been seen again. You can be a selfish little bitch...' He carried on ranting but I still had Valium in my bloodstream. My desire for sleep outweighed any feelings of guilt that I might have harboured had I been truly in my right mind. The night that followed remains a blank in my memory.

The next morning Hubert insisted on my having breakfast in bed. David, it seemed, was coming to interview me at eleven a.m.

'Try and look your best,' said Hubert.

When he'd left my room, I looked at myself in the mirror. I looked like a junkie, dark hollow eyes, sallow skin and lank hair. I ate breakfast quickly, then both showered and bathed. Afterwards, I was liberal with make-up, especially blusher, and thought, once I was dressed, that I looked less like a film extra in *Night of the Living Dead* and more like an over-the-hill PI.

There were two bouquets of flowers on the kitchen table. 'I hope those are not funeral flowers,' I said.

Hubert scowled. 'They are not. One is from Megan and Alvira, and the red roses are from David.'

'Almost worth a near-death experience then,' I said.

'And your car?'

'What about my car?'

'It was found burnt out.'

'Ruth?' I queried, as memories of that strange conversation came back.

'Who is Ruth?'

'Tone – Anthony – was living with her. I think Michael killed her.'

Hubert looked as mystified as I felt. 'There was no one in the car.'

'Thank God,' I murmured.

Hubert left for a funeral and David arrived an hour late and didn't look best pleased.

Jasper went into paroxysms of delight and David spent time fussing him before saying, 'I hope you've learned your lesson.' For a man who'd proposed to me, he'd shown more passion for Jasper, but he did manage to give me a peck and a hug. I smiled and nodded meekly, thinking that, in the circumstances, the less said the better.

'You look worn out,' he said, patting my cheek.

'So would you if you'd been subjected to armfuls of Valium and the ministrations of a deranged nurse.'

'I'm just glad you're OK. Really glad.'

He sounded as if he meant it, and once more I began to warm to him. A decent man was hard to find, I told myself.

'Have you caught Michael?' I asked.

'Not exactly. He flagged down a police car. He's being interviewed at the nick as we speak.'

'Anthony – or Tone – was the rapist, wasn't he?'

'You tell me. You're the one going it alone.'

'You'll probably find the evidence at Kingsfield.'

'We've got men in hard hats strengthening the stairs as we speak.'

'There was an attempt to burn it down. But young Jack rang the fire brigade and it didn't take hold.'

'Why did it take so long to find the van?' I asked.

David smiled, 'Jack gave us a good description but the wrong number plate. We followed the wrong van.'

'How's Grace?' I asked.

David smiled, 'She's fine. I've just come from her place. That's why I'm late. Frank is like a dog with two tails and Grace was a good source of information.'

'Such as?'

'We've been checking the Armstrong family history and Barbara's psychiatric history. Her father Norman spent more time womanizing than farming. Her mother Freda suffered from depression. The accident with the tractor in which Norman was killed caused Barbara tremendous guilt. She had her first mental breakdown then.'

'Was it an accident at all?'

David shrugged. 'Who knows? Far more interesting are the relationships in the family. The one person who guessed the truth was Grace. She'd visited Barbara when she was in hospital following her mother's death. The only other person who visited was Michael.'

'And the significance?'

'The staff noticed the relationship was more than close.'

'Incestuous?'

'Yes.'

'Where did that leave Anthony?'

'Anthony was supposedly an "afterthought" – a menopausal baby – but we can find no evidence of Freda being seen by a doctor for that pregnancy.'

'So you're saying Barbara was Anthony's mother.'

'Yes. Born when she was seventeen.'

'Has she admitted that?'

'Yes. She's realized Anthony's dead and there is no point in lying.'

'And the father?'

'We're doing some DNA tests to establish that. But Grace seems convinced that Michael is the father. He'd have been about fourteen when he fathered Anthony.'

'So, she left Anthony to be looked after by her mother when she did her nurse training?'

'For a year. She didn't qualify. In fact, she was asked to leave because she was showing signs of mental illness. Freda had already had a couple of mild strokes, and much of Anthony's care was down to Michael.'

'What about Norman?'

'It seems that, prior to his death, he'd wanted to employ another young woman to help Freda.'

'Like Ivy, Betty and Alvira?'

'Yes, but of course Freda had learned her lesson by then and the boys and Barbara closed ranks. Norman, it seems, was irresistible to everyone but his wife and family. Barbara has admitted hating him.'

'So it's possible she killed him on purpose?'

'She told the police she was driving the tractor, but there was a suggestion that it was Michael, which seems more likely. Either way, the verdict was accidental death.'

'So then what happened?'

'It seems the family withdrew into themselves. No visitors, no social events, no friends. Anthony never had a girlfriend, until he met Ruth.'

'I thought that Barbara leaving hospital might have been the catalyst.'

'Ruth has finally told us the truth,' said David. 'There was no sexual activity between them, by mutual consent. And as for Anthony not leaving the house at night – they slept in separate rooms and she took sleeping pills.'

'She made a damn good liar. She convinced me.'

'Ruth didn't want to lose him. Women do lie for the men they love.'

'But why choose elderly women? Especially for his first sexual encounter.'

'Who knows? Maybe it was a form of revenge on women who had been involved with his father. Or he had access to their houses? Or he was just a sexual and social inadequate. He loved Ruth because she was so needy, but he didn't want to "sully" her in any way.'

'Ironic, isn't it,' I said, 'that he probably had an Oedipus complex about the wrong woman?'

'Yep. According to Barbara, he didn't know that she was his mother, but she made sure he knew about his father's affairs.'

'So he could well have observed Ivy and Betty and Alvira from afar – doing nothing until he fell in love. And then, unable to make love to the woman he loved, he thought it was payback time.'

'The trouble is,' said David, 'we'll never know for sure. Each one of them was warped.'

While David made coffee, I stared out of the window, past the car park, looking towards Kingsfield. And I thought of the long dull days endured by the three of them. Barbara, desperate for affection, turning to her younger brother. Then the lying and the cover-up and the guilt. It was enough to send anyone mad. The outside world was a danger to them. Grace had become too close, too knowing. Or Barbara had become fond of her and saw her as a genuine replacement for her mother. I'd just been in the right place at the wrong time. Some people,

as the saying goes, 'live lives of quiet des-
peration'. That was certainly true of the
Armstrongs.

'So how long was Barbara actually living in
that attic room?' I asked. 'Surely not for the
six months she was missing?'

'No. She only moved in once she'd
abducted Grace. She's admitted that she was
living with Michael in his cottage and in six
months she didn't go outside. But she did
spend her time persuading and cajoling both
men that they could live back at the farm,
and if she had Grace to look after, it would
be like having their mother with them.'

'Why not improve the downstairs accom-
modation?'

'That would have been far too obvious –
you dumbo,' he said, smiling. 'Anthony, over
the months, managed to create a secret
hideaway that was basic and did at least have
a shower and loo. But, of course, there was
no way all three of them could live perma-
nently in an attic room. And even Barbara
realized they would need to move on,
preferably to somewhere they could all live
together nursing Grace.'

'I didn't see a loo,' I interrupted.

'You were bedridden.'

'True – and drugged to the eyeballs.'

David gave me a look which suggested I
should keep quiet and allow him to con-

tinue. 'Anthony shopped and undoubtedly stole food from the café. We found enough tins and dry food to last for a year.'

'How long did they plan to stay?'

'Who knows,' said David with a shrug. 'Barbara has admitted wanting to keep Grace until she died, which is a chilling thought.'

'Did Michael know Anthony was a rapist?' I asked as David handed me coffee.

'We're not sure yet but according to Barbara he didn't, and she too refuses to believe her gentle son could be a rapist. She only faltered when she heard the names of the raped women. Then a little doubt crept into her voice.'

'Will they go to prison?' I asked.

'Michael, yes, for his part in the abduction. Barbara will probably be sectioned, depending on the psychiatric and social reports.'

We fell silent for a while. 'I'm thinking of giving up the agency,' I said.

David looked up in surprise. 'I know you don't make much money but—'

'It's not that,' I interrupted. 'All I ever do is muddle through. A bit of danger is OK, but next time I have a feeling I'll make one last fatal mistake.'

'Have you told Hubert?'

'No, I'll tell him after Christmas.'

'You could marry me and have babies – at

least two.'

'If I was going to marry anyone,' I said, 'it would be you. Even though you've made no mad passionate declarations of love.'

'I'm more of a doer, and you know how I feel about you.'

'Do I?'

He took my hand and I began following him. 'I could always show you how much,' he said softly.